THE FAMILY I'M IN

THE
FAMILY
I'M IN

SHARON G. FLAKE

Scholastic Press / New York

Library of Congress Cataloging-in-Publication Data available

ISBN 978-1-338-57320-6

10 9 8 7 6 5 4 3 2 1   25 26 27 28 29

Printed in Italy   183

First edition, April 2025

Book design by Elizabeth B. Parisi

To all the young men who have read my work, written to me, or been impacted by my books, thank you. I will be forever grateful to have touched your lives as you have touched mine.

CHAPTER 1

CALEB AND ME are in Miller Park, way back in the woods where nobody can get hurt. It's our favorite place to shoot. "Hurry up, John-John," he says. "I need to pee."

I lift my arms shoulder-level. Lock my elbow. Draw and shoot. Birds fly out the trees like I was aiming for 'em. I would never do anything like that.

"Wish you were as good as me, huh?" I say, watching Caleb run over to some trees. I sit down, holding my bow like somebody gonna steal it. It cost two hundred dollars. I sold a bunch of stuff to get it, 'cause Mom would never let me buy something like this, and my father is cheap. If it got stolen—Well, it better not get stolen.

"Bad enough you run around like Robin Hood shooting arrows," my father said when I asked him to buy it for me. "I'm not going broke paying for nothing like that."

He'd pay for boxing, track, or basketball, he said. "The kind of things boys do in the 'hood."

I was never like other boys in our neighborhood. I can't shoot hoops. Wasn't allowed to hang on the corner or nowhere else, for that matter. Once I got beat up so bad, a girl had to save me. My boy Caleb saved me once too. Nobody but him and I know about it. Now it's my turn to look out for him. His father is sick, bad. Coming to the park to shoot helps him to not think about things. Helps me too, because of my dad. He don't like me, not the way I am.

Me and Caleb watch *Star Wars*—the first one—every couple of months. We know everyone's parts. We do puzzles, watch gladiators fight on television, play video games and baseball, geeky nerd stuff.

My father never said it to my face, but I know what he be thinking about me: *Weird.* One day he's gonna say the wrong thing to me. Then he'll see, I ain't no kid, don't need him telling me what to do, how to act, who to be all the time.

I'm teaching Caleb how to shoot archery. He's bad at it though. But he's the only one from around here that would do this with me. Which means I can't get too mad at him.

"Caleb, watch your stance." I go over to him. "Keep your body and head still. Lift your shooting arm higher. Yeah. Like that. Now, stand on the shooting line like this. Good."

I get out the way and give Caleb room, the way I wish my father would when it comes to me. That he would just step back and let me do my thing.

Caleb misses the target anyhow. Tries again and again. It's his technique, I think. The way he grips the bow. Where he focuses his eyes. I sit down on a tree stump and wait, while Caleb keeps trying.

Dad thinks Caleb's having such a hard time because he wants to be perfect. That he's scared to make a mistake. In middle school, we teased him about cleaning the boys' room. He gets his hair cut every Wednesday. At our last school, he ironed all his school clothes on Sundays to get them ready for the week. He even ironed his ties and polished his sneakers. Who does that?

Since his father got sick, Caleb's been messing up. I don't say nothing to him about it. He's worried, is all, so not his best at things.

I go pick up the fallen arrows. Caleb's went into trees, over bushes. Two did hit the target at least, but not nowhere near mine. I get a bullseye every time.

Loading another one, Caleb brings up my father.

"Do you think he would hire me?"

"You don't want to work for him."

"I need the money . . . bad . . . like yesterday."

Since Caleb's father got sick, he can't work. Caleb's mother doesn't make enough at the hospital to cover all the bills, especially now that their savings are gone. But working for my father—I wouldn't do it. I'd rather pick up trash, which Caleb don't mind doing anyhow—it's like a hobby to him.

Caleb turns to me with the bow still loaded. I back up.

"Point that in another direction."

He aims it at the ground.

"Your father pays good money . . . in cash . . . Everybody knows it."

"You gonna regret it. Remember I said so."

I go next. Pull his arrows out. Stand on the line. Focus on my posture, the position of my feet, my grip and upper body, then draw, aim, and shoot. I hit the bullseye, try not to move in between arrows when I shoot the next two times.

"And the winner is . . ." I put my arms up like Rocky. "Me all the time."

Now Caleb's sitting on the tree stump picking the skin off his fingers. "If I work for your father this summer, I can get my mother and father caught up on their bills."

Most boys in our neighborhood done worked for my dad. Not Caleb. Last summer Caleb started his own business. He planned to mow lawns again this summer, till his dad got sick. Mr. P. had an aneurysm. It busted last year. Surgery took six hours. He was doing physical therapy until the money ran out. Now, three times a week, Caleb and me walk him up the block and back for exercise. It ain't fun or exciting. But it's got to be done. Other things need to be done at their house too. So, we do it.

We look out for each other like that.

It hasn't always been this way.

In middle school, Caleb didn't like me.

I ain't like him either.

High school changed things.

"We should leave," Caleb says, after a couple of hours. He stands up like he got stuck with a pin. Quick. In a hurry.

I keep practicing, pretending it's my father I'm taking down. Mom says to be respectful, because he loves me. But love ain't just buying sneakers and paying child support. It's . . . I don't know . . . letting your kid be who they say they are, not just who you want 'em to be. Yeah, that's it.

Caleb bends down, yawning and picking up trash. "You ready? I have to make dinner for my father. My mom works a double shift at the hospital tonight."

He sticks empty bottles in a plastic bag, picks up soda cans that wasn't even ours.

On the way to his car, Caleb finally talks about something besides his family and finding a job. He starts in about the junior prom. He wants to know who I'm taking. He's got a girlfriend, Maleeka. I got nobody. My father don't like that about me either. He's always saying a boy my age should be dating and should have more girls than he could count. That's something Dad and I agree on. But girls don't like nice boys.

Every time I'm with my dad, he brings up girls, dating, that kind of stuff. I lie to him a lot, because how can you tell your father you never been on a date or been kissed? You can't. You don't. Not if you're Big John's son.

CHAPTER 2

I SEE MY father a lot, but I don't live with him. His wife don't play that. Most times, we end up here at Home Depot, his favorite place on earth. In the plumbing aisle, he tells me how women never could resist us McIntyre men. To prove a point, he walks over to a woman staring up at a toilet in a box near the top shelf.

"Need some help?" Big John don't wait for her answer. He does what he wants, and starts pushing the tall red ladder over to where she is, like she asked him to.

He don't walk up the ladder steps—he runs. Next thing I know, he's carrying that big old box down the steps, easy, like it's a roll of toilet paper. After he puts the toilet in her cart, she tries to give him five dollars.

Dad bends over and rubs his knee. "Keep your money," he says politely, looking over at me. "I'm teaching my son to be a man."

That what he teaching me?

My father's got jokes. He says he knows we look like twins. He even asks her to guess his age. She lies. She's gotta be lying. No way does he look thirty-two—even if he does have muscles in his neck and everywhere else. Three aisles over he's still smiling, rubbing his sore knee.

Dad ran track in high school. Since he turned fifty-two, he says his knee has been bothering him.

He says, "All the girls chased me at your age, you know."

"You told me," I say.

"If it was allowed, I woulda took six girls to junior prom. That's how many asked me."

In high school, Dad had this reputation with girls. They all knew him, wanted him. That's what he tells me anyhow. Now he's got a different kind of reputation.

He's the dude you don't mess with; or don't borrow money from and forget to pay back. The one everybody knows. That everybody wishes they knew because he can hook you up with a set of tires when yours give out. He'll get you a job with somebody who works for the city or speed things up when you trying to get something done but don't know how. I'm bad for his reputation. He told me that after I got jumped and Caleb's girlfriend, Maleeka, stepped in. After that, my father put me in karate school. It didn't last. I don't like to fight. I can't fight. That's just how it is.

Staring hard at me, Dad says, "Take care of your skin, JJ. Girls ain't attracted to no kind of pimples, razor bumps or otherwise." He rubs his smooth chin. "You been to a dermatologist? I pay enough support for you to see whoever you need to." He tells me what I already know: he only uses Noxzema on his face. "It's old-school. That's why I look so young."

Ignoring him, I go up one aisle, down another, almost running. He finds me every time. Three more aisles and I'm still not talking to him. He don't notice. He's talking enough for both of us. Can't stop, seems like.

"Your wife don't let you talk at home, or you just like getting all up in my business?" I ask.

"Some boys got nobody to look out for 'em. Remember that, JJ."

I remember when him, me, and Mom ate dinner every night at the table at the same time, 6:13, because my father is like that, on time or early. Dependable. A family man.

He *was* anyhow. Now he lives six blocks from us with his other family. I hate it when I see him at the basketball court with his wife's son.

When I called him on it, and asked why he never plays ball with me, he said, "You never liked sports."

So, this is what he and I do—shop at Home Depot, eat at diners and restaurants where the waitresses know my middle name and Dad promises to get their husbands and sons jobs.

I'm still mad at Dad for leaving Mom and me, even though it was a couple years ago, and I'm too old to care if I got a father or not. When he was with us, he was a good father, the best.

Char and Maleeka say they wish their dads were alive. That I should take advantage of my time with him. But most fathers like their daughters just the way they are. With sons, it's different. "Step up. Don't let nobody press up on you. Get all the girls you can, *while* you can. Be like me. Make it happen."

CHAPTER 3

IT'S STILL EARLY. I ask Dad to drop me off at Caleb's. When we get there, his father is in a chair on the porch, with a book. It's nice out. Hot for April. Nobody's wearing coats or sweaters. But they got Mr. P. looking like a mummy, wrapped in a blanket from his shoulders to his feet.

After that aneurysm, you never know which Mr. P. you'll meet. The funny one who knows your middle name. Or the one who's sort of depressed, having a hard time walking.

I jump out Dad's truck before it completely stops.

"Hey, Mr. P." I walk up to the porch railing, hang my arms over the side. "I was on my way home." I look back at Dad. Him and Mr. P. wave at each other. When he asks how I'm doing, I roll my eyes. "You know how he is," I say, talking about my father.

Picking up a bookmark, sitting it between pages to hold his spot, takes Mr. P. way longer than it should. But him doing that lets me know he's still trying—today anyhow. His voice trembles sometimes. Other times the words come out fine but stilted. Like now. "We . . . men . . . are slow . . . learners, John. Women mature a long . . . time . . . before we do. Be patient . . . with your father."

I think about Mom. At twenty-one, she bought herself a house. Dad blew forty thousand dollars when he was her age. It was supposed to be for his first business. My grandmother put the house up for collateral to get a bank loan for him. Somebody told Dad they could double his money in twenty-four days. He ain't seen that man since. My grandmother lost her house.

Eleven years later, after he learned his lesson, he bought her another one. Paid for in cash. He ain't rich. We ain't rich. But Dad's good with money now, business and investments too. Ever since he was cheated out of forty thousand dollars, he's been extra careful about anything having to do with business deals. And he always reminds me that if I play my cards right, I'll end up successful, just like him. But what if I don't wanna be *just like him*?

Mr. P. asks me how I'm doing. He knows I'm lying when I bring up all the girls I'm chasing. He smiles anyhow. Winks. Dad beeps the horn. Didn't I tell him I'm walking home? I thought I did. I even reminded him again in the car just in case. I guess he finally remembers. He beeps three times before he drives away.

Mr. P. tells me to be myself. Any girl who doesn't like that, ain't worth having, he says, picking up his book. Right now I'll take any girl I can get. She'd be my starter girlfriend. You know, a practice one. She wouldn't want to be with anybody else after me though.

A little while later, Caleb comes out the house, sitting on the front steps talking about me, him, Maleeka, and Char going to the drive-in movies because it's what Maleeka wants.

I got stuff to do, I tell him. Mom stuff. Things Dad used to do. Her "honey-do" list done turned into a "son-you-better-do-this" list. She's a good mom, which is why I don't complain most times.

"Go . . . John . . . Have fun . . . while you can," Mr. P. says. I guess ain't nothing wrong with his ears.

Last time me and my friends went out, Caleb and Maleeka kissed the whole time. Me and Char couldn't concentrate on the movie.

"Are you going or not?" Caleb asks.

"I'll think about it."

"What else do you have to do?"

"Nothing."

My father would say that is the problem, I got nothing to do and no girl to do it with. He loves to tell me that when he was my age, he wasn't never, ever bored or lonely, 'cause there was always somebody who wanted to be in his company. I like *my* company just fine. Don't mind being by myself all weekend.

"No," I tell Caleb. "I'm not coming. Y'all go to the movies without me. I'm gonna stay home and watch videos."

In my mind, I can hear my father saying it right now.

Stupid.

CHAPTER 4

I HAD A big mouth in middle school. I talked too much, like Dad. Guess I still do. But back then, I didn't let on how I really felt about things. Like how much I liked Maleeka Madison. Maybe I loved her, who knows. Instead of telling her, I teased her, about her skin color, mostly. Which was stupid. She and me both dark skinned, the same color—except I'm short and she's tall as a tree. I thought if *I* talked bad about the way she looked, people wouldn't tease *me*.

It happened a lot in elementary school, but a boy can't complain about stuff like that. By the time I got in middle school, I figured it was somebody else's turn to get picked on.

Maleeka and Caleb been liking each other since forever. It don't bother me. I'm over her now anyway. But sometimes, every once in a while, I wonder if I had treated her differently, would she maybe be mine now? Would Dad still be ashamed of me?

Me and Maleeka are both in book club. Usually, I wait for her here at the window in a rocking chair. There's a basketball game going on across the yard. Seniors playing tennis on a court. Teachers in the garden with students. I still can't believe I go to this school. It ain't nothing like McClenton Middle or the first high school I ended up at. The walls here are all glass, floor to ceiling. No matter where you sit, the sun finds you. That's why I got on sunglasses. They don't like us to wear 'em in the building, but oh well.

I left my old high school after they opened this school up to boys. Plus, I was tired of getting beat up. It's my big mouth, a school counselor told me. "You can't keep it shut," she said. True.

Even though I talked too much, I didn't fit in, which meant I hung out at the library a lot. I ate breakfast and lunch there. That's how me and Caleb got to be friends. In middle school, I knew he didn't like me. He's a nerd. A geek. Me too. At our other high school, he got picked on as much as I did once he decided to run for class president. Boys like us ain't always appreciated, except at a school like this.

It's in our neighborhood, a charter school. They'll give us a four-year scholarship when it's time for college. All we got to do is keep our grades up. At least that's one thing I do better than my father. Even he'll admit it.

"Ready?" Maleeka walks up behind me. She takes my sunglasses off and puts 'em on. "How do I look?"

Beautiful, I say in my head.

She's changed out of her school clothes into a short black dress, the kind you wear someplace special. Her mother and her mom's fiancé are taking her to an expensive restaurant after book club, she tells me.

Dudes walk by staring down at me, looking Maleeka up and down, smiling like she a new pair of Jordans they'd steal if they could. Tall with a 'fro, Vaseline legs, pretty chocolate-brown skin. Maleeka could have any boy she wants. Nerd Caleb is who she wants. Ten points for us nerds.

We pass the music room. Violins and trumpets, drums and French horns play so loud they hurt your ears. Trying to talk over them, Maleeka asks if I'm going to the junior prom.

"Maybe."

Caleb showed up in physics last week carrying six roses and twelve balloons. He got down on one knee and read a poem he wrote for her, then invited Maleeka to the junior prom. Girls took pictures and videos. Said they wished it was them. I lent him half the money. You can't come empty-handed to ask the prettiest girl in school to the junior prom.

"I was thinking about asking Ashley," I tell Maleeka. "But you know how her mother is." I open the library door for Maleeka. Soon as we get inside, the librarian says for anybody with snacks to bring 'em over to the table where she's setting up.

I wouldn't bring nothing if it wasn't for Mom. She's got "book club" marked on a calendar. I woke up this morning and there it was—a jumbo bag of cheddar cheese popcorn in my backpack. I pull it out. The librarian empties it into a bowl half-filled with pretzels. Right then, Miss Saunders comes in. She was our middle school teacher. A lot of kids hated her then. She's a vice principal now. Part of her job is to recruit boys, make sure we graduate on time. She's the reason why I'm here. She even got Maleeka to transfer schools.

I go over to see her, putting my arm around her shoulder. "Is that a cheeseburger you got in that bag, Miss Saunders? Fries? Smells like it." I rub my stomach. "I ate lunch, but I'm still hungry."

Char walks in. I follow Miss Saunders over to her. "You

forgot this." She gives her the bag. "Your sister brought it by. She has to work late."

I ask Miss Saunders if she's got extra food in her office for me. She tells me to come by after book club. "I want to talk to you about something anyhow. A summer job. And bring Caleb."

I don't want a job. But I don't say anything. When it's almost time for book club to start, I go sit down across from Ashley, who waves at me.

"Hi, John," she says.

I swear, when she says my name, I hear music. "Hey."

She's the first girl I ever saw who wears skirts way past her knees. And walks like she got clouds under her feet. "Did you read all the chapters?" she asks.

My head goes up and down, because after I say her name it's like my throat closes. And my words get trapped. "Yeah . . . yeah . . . yeah." I sit up straight. "You going to junior prom?" I say to Ashley. It comes out too loud. Everyone's looking at me now. Some girls laugh. It's hard being the only boy in book club.

Ashley seems sad when she tells me that her mother won't allow her to go to parties or dances, or other people's houses.

I don't do most of those things either. My father wants me to though. It's just that I'm in the house most of the time unless I'm with Caleb. But how you tell a girl that? You can't. You don't. It don't sound cool. Not cool at all. And cool in this neighborhood goes a long way.

CHAPTER 5

ASHLEY'S MOTHER IS the only school secretary we got. She talks nice to our faces. But everybody knows how she feels about boys at this school, especially. Behind our backs, she's got plenty to say. None of it good.

Nervous, I go into the office and ask how she's feeling. She was out most of the week because of a sore throat.

"I'm better. Good. Thank you for asking. You're such a nice boy, John-John."

"I'm here because Miss Saunders is expecting me." I take some chocolate candies from the bowl on the counter.

She gets out her seat, comes over to where I'm at, and sticks her hand out. I give her what she wants, the wrapper from the candy.

"What do your parents think about what happened at school last week?" she says on her way back to her desk.

Last weekend, a boy rode a motorcycle into the building, up and down the hall on the first floor. Before he got caught, he broke the case with the awards and trophies and spray-painted the office door. Police came. Firemen rolled in. Reporters too. Nothing like that ever happened at our school before.

"It's the neighborhood," Ashley's mother says, sitting down. She taps a pencil on her desk and tells me how some days she thinks about transferring Ashley somewhere else. "But there's so much to like here. A beautiful building. The curriculum and after-school activities. Good, caring teachers. I just wish it was in another location."

I want to ask her, *What about us?*

Kids who live here. Don't we deserve good things? Anyhow, this school wasn't put here for Ashley. She got admitted because her mom works here. Otherwise, you need our zip code to attend. Ashley told Maleeka her mother only took the job so she could get scholarship money for college.

Ashley's mother hits the buzzer to let me in Miss Saunders's office. Soon as I'm in there, Miss Saunders offers me a sandwich. Plus two bags of Doritos.

"Thanks."

I'm eating before I get to my seat. Half my sandwich is gone when I ask if she had a daughter, would she let her date me.

It takes her too long to answer, so I start making jokes. Miss Saunders stops me. Says she has high hopes for me at this school and in life. Sitting down, she pats my hand. "The right girl will come, John."

My mother says that. But when will *the right girl come?*

Miss Saunders tells me that most likely, the right girl for me is already at this school. "It only takes one."

I think about Ashley, who is my height with pretty brown skin and big eyes. Her lips, I dream about kissing them.

Miss Saunders says I've grown a lot since middle school. "You still think you're a comedian. But there's a sincerity about you that wasn't there when you were much younger."

Miss Saunders wrote me a really good letter of recommendation for this school. Char read it, said she ain't know Miss Saunders could lie that good. I laughed right along with Char, because on paper, I look way better than I do in real life. So, it did seem like it wasn't all true. I'm an A student, so it's for real. And I came here with two years' worth of volunteer experience. But this summer, I'm not doing nothing, *nada*, except sleeping in late, eating everything in the house.

She walks over to the door to tell Ashley's mom to page Caleb. Like magic, he shows up before the announcement. Right away, Miss Saunders offers him a sandwich.

"No, thank you. I'm not hungry."

"I ate at chess club," I say, imitating him.

She sits a big box of chocolate-almond candy bars in front of him anyhow. I take what she's offering. Not him, not at first.

In three months, it'll be summer, Miss Saunders says, like we don't know. It's her job to make sure boys at this school are employed if we want to be. The other vice principal works with the girls.

Caleb says he needs to make more than minimum wage. Him and Dad keep missing each other, so he still hasn't talked to him.

Miss Saunders asks about his father, and his mom too. Everybody's fine, Caleb says a lot.

My father is right about one thing. Don't nothing happen in this neighborhood he don't know about. "I heard they might lose the house," Dad said one day. "Be a shame if they did."

It wouldn't make sense, Caleb tells Miss Saunders, to

work for a little bit of money when his mother and father need a whole lot of help.

Miss Saunders acts like she understands. Then she brings up his grades. "In physics you went from an A to a B-minus, and an A-plus to a C-minus in history."

She makes him look at her.

"Mr. Maccabee says you could end up with a D in English if this keeps up." He'd told Caleb he could bring up his grade by doing a special project. "Why didn't you do it?" Miss Saunders wants to know.

"I just didn't."

She leaves him alone to pick on me, asking what kind of job I'm looking for.

"You know my father, Miss Saunders. He's making me work for him." I'm lying. I wouldn't work for my dad for all the money in the world. This summer, I'm gonna sleep till three thirty every day. Eat cereal for breakfast, lunch, and dinner. Watch all the movies I missed this year. Play video games. Go to as many archery competitions as I can. Get me a girl. 'Cause that's what summer is for.

Caleb stands up. "Are you done with me, Miss Saunders?"

You got to know Caleb. He's respectful, always. Never breaks the rules or nothing. But he's been wildin' out on people lately, even me. Even his girlfriend. I think he gave Maleeka those flowers to make up for things.

Miss Saunders stands up too. "I put in a call to your mother, Caleb."

"She works a lot of overtime. You can tell me and I'll tell her."

He's on his way out her office when she stops him. "I used

to work for a corporation before I got into education. Maybe I can shake a few bushes and find you something that pays more."

In the meantime, she asks what else can she do to help.

He don't say nothing.

"Your school family is always here to help, Caleb," she tells him.

"Really? Then why is my family about to lose our—oh, forget it."

He leaves the office without me.

I get to him fast. He ignores me all the way to his car. On the way home, I ask Caleb if he wants to go do target practice.

"Nope."

"Wanna come in my house and play video games?"

"No."

"What about the drive-in movies on Saturday?" I finally say. "I'll go if you go."

He turns down the music. "Thanks, John-John." Then he calls Maleeka.

CHAPTER 6

I KEEP TELLING myself this ain't a date, even though I paid for Char's popcorn and everything else she's over there eating.

Char and me are in the back seat talking about the movie, laughing at the same time. We shake our heads at them two up front. Caleb and Maleeka practically sitting in each other's laps. Their heads touch. They kiss a whole lot. I went to the drive-in bathroom pavilion twice already 'cause I don't wanna see all that. Only, it keeps happening.

"Hey." Char shakes her popcorn bag. "They give you refills, right?"

"Yeah." I open my door.

She opens hers. "Maleeka. Caleb. Y'all want something?" I slam the door shut.

"Nope." Caleb's hand is on her shoulder, rubbing it.

"I'm full." Maleeka's eyes stay on the screen.

Me and Char walk over gravel, duck to keep from messing up other people's views. It feels like miles from here to the concession building. We don't talk most of the way. Then Char gets a message on her phone and laughs.

"Read this." She gives me her phone, and we both end up laughing.

"This what you girls be doing? You know that ain't right, Char."

"Well—maybe his breath do smell like cheese doodles."

"She's still kissing him, I bet."

"Hot and heavy, for real." Char laughs.

"I kept thinking . . . I don't want to be here. I don't wanna see this."

"Right!" Char says.

I open the concession building door and walk in behind her. My wallet is out by the time we get in line. I ask if she wants something to drink. Refills ain't free, they cost.

"I'll pay," I say.

Char looks around, like always. "No. I got this."

Once her bag is full, she fills up her cup. We walk over to another counter where she puts butter on her popcorn. She's not paying attention, so the butter ends up on her shirt and fingers.

I help her clean up, one finger at a time. "You owe me, Char."

"Sorry, John-John."

"Well, I ain't say you owed me an apology. But I'll take it."

On the way back, she explains why she's apologizing. It's for telling me last week how terrible I treated everybody in middle school.

"You mean, I wasn't mean to Maleeka and Desda back then?"

"Yeah, you was."

Walking backward, she stares at me. "But you not the same John-John like I'm not the same Charlese Jones."

Char quits walking and stares up at the sky. "One, two, three . . ."

I look up. "You counting stars?"

"Yeah. Six, seven . . ."

There's thousands up there. The moon ain't so bright so you can see 'em all. "You know some of those aren't stars, they're actually planets," I tell her.

"I know."

We stop under a tree. Not that we talk about much. But we stay awhile. We're here so long, Maleeka calls Char asking when we coming back.

"You should draw a picture of me," I tell Char. "Me all by myself."

Char got in our school because of Miss Saunders and her drawing skills. When she's nervous, she colors. I notice sometimes. Maleeka got in because she writes well. If you want to go to our charter school, you got to be strong in something to qualify for admission. I'm good at talking. For real. I want my own talk show. My own network. Putting that dream in writing, giving real good examples during my interview, making a video with Maleeka's help—that got me in. Studying hard is gonna keep me there. Being a boy sure don't hurt none. They always want gifted boys.

"I knew you would make me pay for this drink one way or the other, John-John." Char gives me a big old smile. "But, okay, I'll draw your picture. Where? When?"

"Next week," I tell her. "In school, after school. It don't matter. I know you volunteer a lot."

Char helps out at a program for people who been through

some hard things. Most are runaways, like she was that time. Some been abused. It happened to her too. Some are depressed. I was depressed after my parents divorced.

I'm always telling her she needs to relax. Slow down, have more fun like me. She can't, she says. She's got to make up for lost time. "Be the girl my mother and father woulda wanted me to be."

They would be proud of her. I'm proud of her, only I don't say so. A boy can't tell a girl everything. Even if she's a good friend. Otherwise, she could use it against him. Because sometimes friends stop being friends. Then where you at? Screwed if you told 'em something you didn't want the whole world to know.

We watch the movie screen, the sky, each other. She's the one who finally says we should get back to the car. Soon as we start walking, Char points left. "Ain't that your dad?"

CHAPTER 7

MY FATHER'S GOT popcorn and a big box of chocolate M&M's in his hand. His wife is carrying the drinks, extra-large. Him and her are alike. They talk a lot, know everybody. Even Char. Soon, they're right in front of us.

Dad's wife, Sheila, and me got nothing to say to each other unless somebody else besides my dad is around. Then she acts like she likes me when I know she don't.

"How are things with you, JJ?"

I told her to call me John-John, but she's still saying "JJ."

Char's got me by the arm, like I belong to her. "He good. Right, John-John?"

Dad and his wife don't see the heel of her sneaker stepping hard on my big toe, trying to keep me in line.

"I'm alright."

My father smiles. Sheila brings up the junior prom. She wants to know if Dad ever showed me any of his moves. Why would he mention it to her? Why would he talk about it to anybody?

They put their stuff on the hood of an old Buick in the parking lot, with nobody in it. "Your father's still got it." Sheila's shoulders start moving. Her feet and arms get to working. Dad starts fast dancing with her, turning her in circles like there's music playing. Stones get kicked and hit me and Char in the legs.

I look around to see who's watching. Dad's wife says she wishes she knew him in high school so he could have taken her to the prom. He puts his arm over her shoulder. Next thing I know, he's hugging her like he ain't never gonna let go.

"John-John didn't tell you?" Char stands close. "He's taking me to junior prom."

My father acts like she said I won the lottery or got a new car for free. "My boy!"

Sheila tells him not to be so loud. He walks up to me with his hand out.

I shake his hand just to get it over with.

"Told you the boy kind of shy." He slaps me on the back and smiles at Sheila. "But I been working on him."

She brings up her son, Giovanni. He's six. Rubbing her pregnant stomach, she says this one is a girl. They're trying to think up names. If I come up with one, I should let her know, she tells me. "And drop by the house sometime."

She looks at Dad and tells him she'll meet him at the car, then leaves.

"She don't seem so bad," Char says quietly to me.

I tell my father that I gotta leave too.

Dad is always reminding me that lots of marriages don't work out, which is what happened with him and Mom.

"But you'll always be my son," he says.

"Tell that to your wife."

"You ain't no kid. We divorced when you were what, in ninth grade? Seems like you'd be over it by now."

Once, after I got in an argument with my father over the phone and started crying, a dude at my old high school named Malik said, "You half-grown, John-John. Why you still crying and mad about it? Just get over it."

I kicked Malik in the leg. Almost broke it. He broke my thumb. We both got suspended.

CHAPTER 8

BY THE TIME I get to book club, I got on new sneakers. Dad dropped 'em off at school.

He had me pulled out of class so he could give 'em to me. I met him at his truck. At first, I turned him down. Because I don't want to lie to Mom. Already this year, he got me six pairs without telling her he was spending that kind of money.

"That's enough," Mom told him the last time.

"But you can't ever have too many pair of sneakers," Dad had said.

That's one thing Dad and I agree on.

At school when Dad brought the sneakers, he handed them over and said, "Tell him he's got it."

I didn't know what he meant.

"Caleb . . . He called and asked me for a job."

Caleb won't like any job Dad gives him. My father pays good but works you hard. Mom always says she could not work for him again, ever. He was her boss until two years before the divorce.

Ashley can't keep her eyes off my feet. I notice that as soon as I step into the library.

"Like 'em?"

We can't wear sneakers during school, but after classes end

and clubs begin, it's cool, so I put the sneakers on for book club.

"These cost two-fifty. Maybe three." I sit down across from her.

She smiles. I smile back.

In my mind, I say, *Ashley, would you like to go to the junior prom?*

I don't know why I'm bothering to ask, even if it is only in my head. Ashley's mother wouldn't allow it anyhow.

Today, some girl stood on the table and sang to a boy about how she wanted him to go to the junior prom with her. It's like everybody's going, except me.

I get my book out. Ashley repeats what she told me the other day, some of it anyhow. She sort of smiles at me when she says she really would like to go.

Ashley jokes about being a bad dancer, and we all laugh.

"John." Ashley waits until the book discussion starts to say, "I think you're nice."

"I think you're nice too." I feel my throat dry up. "Ashley?"

"Yeah?"

"Ah . . . nothing."

The library door opens. Maleeka walks in and sits down at the only empty seat. The one beside me. I wanna tell her she just missed a girl flirting with me. But I keep my big mouth shut. Next thing I know, Maleeka's crying.

Her mom's had cancer a couple of times. I figure it's back.

"Sorry, Maleeka," I say.

The librarian wants to know what's wrong. Maleeka tells her it's nothing. Char walks over to Maleeka, hugging her right along with me.

"You okay? Your mother alright?" Char asks.

Everybody's watching and listening. Maleeka finally smiles. "It's not bad news."

Char wipes Maleeka's cheeks with both palms.

"The doctor said—"

There she is crying again. Harder this time. I run to get a napkin. Jog back, and hand it to her. Wiping her face, Maleeka tells us her mother's cancer is in remission, and there ain't no more sign of cancer.

Even Ashley stands up and hugs her. The whole group does, all at the same time.

"Now she can get married." Maleeka sits down with Char, holding her hand like they a couple. Her mother's been engaged for a while. She wouldn't set a date until they told her the cancer was gone.

"Now we can go shopping for wedding dresses. I'm a bridesmaid."

Someone asks Maleeka if she's ready for a stepfather. "Sure," I hear her say. "Mr. Porter is nice. And we both like reading and books." She holds up our book club pick, *If Beale Street Could Talk* by James Baldwin. "He read this before I did."

Maleeka's new stepdad, he'll change. Not in a good way. Her mother will too. They all do once they remarry. I wish I could tell that to Maleeka, but she's happy, letting girls take pictures with her. Telling us how much her mother's fiancé likes Caleb. How easy it is to talk to him. So, I don't say nothing. She'll find out soon enough. Just like I did.

CHAPTER 9

ONE DAY DAD gives me sneakers. The next day he gives me problems.

We at Home Depot when he brings up junior prom. My father mentions his friend's kids, how they been dating since middle school. I can't help but lie. "I already turned three girls down. I got standards, Dad."

He likes that a lot, I can tell.

I'm handsome like him. He tells me I better be choosy like him if I wanna end up with the best . . . like him. But then he realizes what he's saying.

"Oh, um, your mom . . . ah, yeah, she's a good woman. A great mother. Nobody's better."

"Not even your new wife?"

"I only pick the best. I lucked up, I guess, and did it twice. Look and learn, JJ. Look and learn." He takes pills out of his pocket and swallows them without water. His knee is acting up again. "They wanna do surgery. Cut me from here to here." He bends over to show me. "They must think I was born yesterday."

"But, Dad, your knee hurts . . . all the time. Mom says maybe they should replace it."

"Your mother talks too much."

CHAPTER 10

YESTERDAY OVER THE intercom, Ashley's mother said for boys interested in summer employment to come to the office at the end of the day. Caleb and me ain't go. He's already got a job. I don't want one. A little while ago, Ashley's mom got on the intercom again. This time she singled me and Caleb out. Just us two. You know we on our way now.

Caleb stops at the bathroom next door to the office. Standing next to me, he tells me he took the job with my father. I never mentioned it. For real, I just forgot. Anyhow, it don't matter to me one way or the other if he wants to ruin his summer.

"Your dad said I can work as many hours as I want."

"Don't they got child labor laws against that?" I crack myself up.

Getting serious, I ask if he's alright. I asked him the same thing at lunch. He didn't talk to none of us while we ate—not even Maleeka, who was sitting in his lap.

Caleb smiles, but it's a pretend one. Zipping up, he says, "I'm good."

He goes to the sink and turns on the water. Splashing cold water in his face, he rubs his eyes. They're red. They stay red. Caleb yawns a bunch of times and leaves without me.

I wash my hands, put ChapStick on, and walk out like

I'm the cutest dude in this building—'cause I am. Soon as I open the front door to the main office, there she is—Ashley Brownley Dickerson. She sure looks pretty. Even a long dress with long sleeves can't hide it.

"Hi," I manage to say.

"Hey, John." She's behind the counter, standing next to her mother's desk. "Mom, this is—"

"I know John-John." She picks something off Ashley's sleeve. Lint, I think.

"You two boys can go in. Miss Saunders is waiting."

I should leave, but I don't. Caleb goes into Miss Saunders's office without me. Ashley's mom smiles like maybe she thinks I want something else from her.

"What are your plans for the summer, Ashley?" I say with my voice shaking.

Her mom answers, like I asked her the question. Ashley enjoys shopping, her mom tells me. So she guesses she'll be doing that. Plus, she's been applying for summer jobs. But she'll volunteer if she can't get one.

Ashley usually stands up straight. She's sort of bent over when she tells me, "I want to be a weather reporter. To work at WPIZ TV this summer."

Her mother's lips get tight. "It's hard to get those jobs."

"I'd do anything . . . even sweep floors."

Her mom starts picking up papers, putting 'em down, hard. "Don't you have an appointment, John-John?"

"I, um, yeah."

Halfway to Miss Saunders's office, I turn around. "I could see you as a reporter, Ashley. Bet you would do a great job."

CHAPTER 11

THINKING IT OVER, I go back to Miss Saunders's office to join Caleb. I don't want to leave him on his own. Miss Saunders can be a lot.

We're standing across from her desk, listening.

"A job came up, and I think you two will be perfect for it," Miss Saunders tells us.

I look at Caleb. She sits on the edge of her desk. Him and me still standing. The place where she volunteers twice a month has a truck, she tells us. They had it remodeled. Turned it into a bookmobile a few years ago. "They need two workers."

"What happened to the good-paying job downtown?" I ask her.

"We could kill two birds with one stone. Get you two employed and help the community." Miss Saunders talks about how many kids around here could benefit from a bookmobile. The library near us closed. That makes it a challenge for students to keep their skills up during the summer, she tells us.

I feel bad that some kids won't have no books to read. But I still don't want the job.

Caleb asks how much it pays.

And he wants to know exactly what time he'd start work and stop for the day.

Not sure why he's asking, since he already got a job.

All the details haven't been worked out, Miss Saunders says. But she did tell them they need to hire young men from around here. It'll put money in our pockets that way, she tells us. "And you'll be role models to the younger boys."

"But I don't need a job," I say, looking at Caleb. "Him either. Tell her, Caleb."

She keeps talking. "The job pays a dollar fifty above minimum wage."

Caleb asks about weekends. And what time we'd get off for lunch.

Under my breath, I tell Caleb to stop saying *we*.

Miss Saunders gives him the hours and the days. Caleb would be at work with my father then. And this bookmobile truck don't do weekends. She said so herself.

Sitting down, Caleb takes a piece of paper out and writes down numbers. He's figuring out how much money he'll make working both jobs. Miss Saunders offers us cold water, soda, or iced tea. She's on her way to the refrigerator to get the drinks before we say if we want anything or not. I ask for two bags of chips, two cans of soda, and anything Caleb doesn't want.

"Don't be greedy." Caleb is serious.

I point. "She's got a big box on the top shelf."

Caleb only wants water. Miss Saunders asks if he would like a soft pretzel with it. "I can warm it in the microwave."

Caleb licks his lips, then rubs his mouth. I can hear his stomach growl.

"Okay, thanks, Miss Saunders."

Me getting on him about not hardly eating is working, I

think. At lunch today, he ate everything on his plate. With so much going on with his dad, Caleb doesn't have an appetite lately. I get it. "But you still have to eat," Maleeka and me tell him whenever we get the chance.

Miss Saunders sits down on her desk again. "I'll need an answer about the jobs soon. If you turn me down, I'll need to recruit other boys."

"Miss Saunders—" I start.

"I'll speak with your mother, John-John."

"My mother!"

I'm a little too immature to make these kinds of decisions on my own, she tells me. Her hand squeezes my shoulder. "I want to make sure you're making the best choice. And not being impulsive by saying no so quickly."

"Caleb and me are the same age." I ask if she'll be talking to *his* mom or dad.

She don't answer. Which means no.

"I gotta go, Miss Saunders," I say.

I get to the door quick, slamming it on my way out. Only, I forgot about Ashley and her mother. I apologize to them right away.

"Nobody's perfect." That's all Ashley gets to say, before her mother interrupts her.

"I thought better of you, John-John. I really did." Then she mumbles something about boys from our neighborhood.

CHAPTER 12

"I JUST DON'T want it," I said to Mom soon as I got in the house.

Miss Saunders called about the job. I went straight upstairs to my room. Now Mom's yelling for me to come downstairs and eat. If I wasn't hungry, I wouldn't go.

Me and Mom pray first. Then she fills our plates. I handle the drinks. Neither one of us is talking much. That's good because I don't wanna get asked about things I don't want to talk about, like a summer job and the lawn needing to be cut.

We're eating dessert—blueberry-apple pie Mom made herself—when she brings up the bookmobile truck again. "Miss Saunders says she could really use your help with it this summer."

No way am I driving around the neighborhood in a van trying to get kids to read who don't want to read, I tell her.

Mom puts her fork down. "Don't say that. Kids will read things that interest them." She sounds like the librarian at school.

They keep books at the shelter where Mom works. "Children love to sit and read to the animals. It's how we teach 'em to have empathy and care for their pets."

Mom is the secretary at the animal shelter. That's why we got five dogs.

"Down." I give Macon the evil eye. He's a greedy German

shepherd, old like all the animals Mom brings home. Nobody wants 'em when they stop being cute and little. "Here. Now, go away." I tear a piece of white bread and throw it over Macon's head.

"You're good with animals, JJ. And kids. Think about the bookmobile. Boys need to know that books ain't just for girls to read."

I don't need to think about it. I'm not doing it. Besides wanting to do nothing all summer, working on a book truck ain't a good look for me. "Ain't you tired of me getting teased, Mom?" I touch my chin and my cheek, checking for bumps. "I am."

She shakes her head. I rip more bread into pieces. Throw it over my shoulder right when sirens pass by the house. The dogs go wild and forget about the food. They whine and moan, run to the door like they wanna open it to see where the fire is.

"You always liked going to the school library."

I pick at food stuck between my teeth, wash it down with iced tea made by me, and think about me at the library. I started going because I had to, not because I wanted to. It was the only place I didn't get bullied at my last high school. I go in the mornings at school now mostly because I'm used to it. But I don't like books enough to be stuck on a truck where everybody in the neighborhood can see me. That would make them think that what they already believe about me is true—that I got no game, no cool, nothing.

I say it again. "I don't need a job."

Mom sits back in her chair. "Well, you have to work some-where. Come up with a plan by next week, JJ."

A plan? By next week? I stand up to clear the table. "We ain't out of school for a long time yet."

If I think I'm hanging around doing nothing all summer, I'm mistaken, she says. Following behind me carrying plates and forks in her hands, Mom asks what Caleb is doing this summer. I don't say. She knows not to ask me to work at the shelter. I'm around dogs too much now. Bet I smell like dog sometime. How many did we have last month? Six, I think. Mom started off as a volunteer. They liked her so much they hired her. No way would I wanna work with them and live with 'em too.

In the kitchen, we do what we do every night. Wash dishes together. Soon as I turn on the hot water, the house phone rings. It's Dad. "Go ahead." She turns off the water. "I wanna talk to him about them sneakers anyhow. And don't ask how I know. It's my house and anything coming in or going out, I make it my business to know about."

Dad needs to change the time we meet tomorrow, he tells her, after complaining how I don't answer my own phone. Mom brings up my sneakers again.

"Buy the boy sneakers," Dad says, "or blow the money on numbers and lottery tickets, or another pair of shoes my wife don't need. Which is better?"

"Discussing it with me first is better." She turns on the water and squirts dish liquid in the sink. "I'm raising him to be responsible."

"And I'm not?" The bubbles grow. Dad's voice gets deeper when he says if she wants me to be more responsible she ought to let me come work for him.

"He don't want to."

Families all over this neighborhood trust their boys to him, he tells her. "But not my son's mother. How that look?"

She don't get to answer. He talks over her . . . a lot.

"Men turn boys into men. Women can't do that." He brings up Mr. Junior's sons. They're triplets.

"Why you always have to compare him to other boys? He's his own person, you know."

I start washing. He mentions me being in the book club. Turns out, Mom told him even though she said she absolutely wouldn't.

He talks about boys around here getting basketball scholarships, making all-American in high school, starting their own businesses. "And what they got in common? They all worked for me. You got our son over there washing dishes I bet."

A plate slips out her wet hands and breaks. "Look what you did!" she says, like he can see what happened.

"I know boys. I work with 'em every day."

I pick up the pieces. Walk to the can under the window and throw 'em away. I sweep up, leaving the room with my hands still wet.

"Can't JJ just be who he is?" I hear Mom say. "Does he have to be like everybody else's son you know? When you were his age—"

"I wasn't no thug. I was—"

"I didn't say you were," Mom says.

I go upstairs to my room and slam the door. Their words find me anyhow, even with two pillows over my head and a headache big as New York City. They're still at it an hour later. Me, I'm lying on the bed thinking about Ashley. If we ever get married, it won't be anything like this. No arguments. No name-calling. And no kids. Grown-ups don't mean to, but a lot of what they say or do to kids sticks like fillings in your teeth. Even if you go to therapy. Even if they apologize. What they did to you is still there.

CHAPTER 13

THE FIRST NIGHT Dad and his new wife moved into their house, I came by. I been here a bunch of times since, not that they know. It's always at night while they are asleep or upstairs. I came after the fight last night too. Just sat on their front porch in the dark, staring. Him and her the type that don't put blinds up at the windows. Just curtains, sheer. Like they want the whole world to see 'em together. That first night, I went to see for myself why what he had with her was better than what he had with Mom and me. It ain't better, far as I can see. Just different. A different address. A different family. A baby coming. He always wanted a big family. Mom couldn't have any more children. Maybe that's why we got a house full of dogs.

Dad never caught me out here. Guess I'm tired this time; I end up falling asleep sitting up on their porch. When I wake up, there's a blanket covering me. And he's sitting beside me holding a baseball bat.

"I don't want to talk about it," I say, standing up.

"We don't have to. Do me a favor though. Next time, knock on the door. Come in the house. We got extra beds, a comfortable couch."

"She don't want me."

"I want you. Let that be enough for now."

I stick my feet in sneakers I don't remember taking off. And give him back his blanket. "Dad."

"Yeah."

"Please don't talk to Mom like that, alright?"

"Like what?"

"Hollering at her like you did last night. I don't like it."

I'm on the sidewalk when he stands up and says, "You don't like it. You a man now?"

"Just don't holler at her."

"She asked you to tell me that?"

"No."

"Then she ain't got a problem with me. You do."

"I can't talk to you."

I walk home slow, like I got all night. It's dark out, no moon. Pitch-black when I get to our block. It wasn't when I left. The streetlight is out.

CHAPTER 14

CALEB CALLED. HE said he needed to shoot something. Lights in the park get turned off at ten p.m. We stay until then. I think he feels guilty sometimes when he gets tired of helping out at home. But he don't never complain even though he's got a right to. Mr. P. would understand, I told Caleb tonight.

"I'm good," he says, faking a smile. "Coming out here . . . helps . . ."

". . . you get used to losing?"

"Not that."

I'm serious when I say, "It makes you forget about things, huh?"

He doesn't answer.

"It helps *me* forget some things," I say, "like how everybody is going to the junior prom with somebody, except me."

He shoots. Shoots again. Couldn't hit the bullseye if you paid him. I don't think I'd wanna come if I couldn't.

CHAPTER 15

ONE DAY MY father's gonna work hisself to death. I told Caleb that yesterday on the way home, right before my father called me. Instead of going to Home Depot tonight, he wanted me to help him unload one of his trucks. I'm lying down in the grass in front of his building, watching him.

"Hard work gets you money and muscles," Dad says, passing me. Then he tells me to get up and help him finish emptying the truck.

It ain't long before I'm sweating going back and forth—stopping, breathing like I got asthma. Dad's almost skipping. Can't stop talking. "See . . . this is how you do it, son." He empties the rest of the truck by himself. Pulls up his sleeve, showing off his muscles.

My father guts houses. He's got a couple of crews. A couple of garages too. He keeps equipment for his businesses there. Dad has lots of other things in there too like drills, hatchets, all kinds of ladders and saws (some electric), and hammers, racks, wheelbarrows, doorknobs. He'll let you buy or rent things at a discount.

He dumps a sack of seeds on the lawn. "I don't know, JJ . . . about being no father to a girl."

Who was talking about girls?

"I know how to raise boys . . ."

I keep my mouth shut.

". . . You didn't turn out too bad . . . I don't think." Him and the sun look down on me. "Proud of you, son."

I never hear that much.

Dad starts naming the things I did but forgot about a long time ago. Me coming in first at a YMCA swim meet when I was eight. Me coming in second in the spelling bee three years in a row in elementary school. Me being his son because John McIntyre don't make no punks.

I stand up, wiping my hands on my pants. "Um, you sure . . . it's a girl . . . Sonograms can be wrong sometimes; I heard it anyhow."

"JJ, I saw her."

I wonder how he'll treat a girl. Sometimes I think he treats her son better than me; not that I'm jealous or nothing. I got Mom. She's got me. And he's a little kid.

Dad's on his way to the truck. "Better get up. The junkyard is closed tomorrow."

Lying on the lawn, I close my eyes. "Nah, I'm good. I'll walk home."

"JJ. I'm here. Let's do this thing, okay?" He's in the truck when he hollers, "You coming?"

"Why you in such a good mood?"

They gave him a shot in his knee, he says. "I feel brand-new."

I ride in the back by myself. He used to always let me ride back here, even when I was little. Mom never liked it. You bounce around not strapped in. Sitting with my legs up, I hold on to the side of the truck. From back here, I can hear my father singing with the radio. It's a loud, bumpy ride. Dogs bark. People on porches playing cards talk loud, laugh loud, cuss loud. I'm watching, listening, hoping I get to live here the rest of my life.

Dad brakes so hard the back of my head hits the glass separating him from me. I stand up, rubbing my head. Dad's out the truck, yelling at a little boy he almost hit.

Martin is always out by himself, rain or snow. It's like he's homeless or a pet people feed, let in to get warm, and forget about in between. Sometimes even the mailman walks him home. My father reaches into his pocket. Pulls out his wallet. Takes out a dollar. "Here. Buy yourself some candy tomorrow." He opens the passenger door. "Let's go home, little man."

Right then, the street fills up with motorcycles. Some riders stand up on their way up the street. One man's riding with both his legs in the air. A couple of 'em beep at Dad on their way by. My father waves and tells me like I don't know that everybody in this city knows who Big John is.

Martin gets out four blocks up. "Thank you, Mr. John." Dad waits until he's in the house before we leave.

It happens again in the next block. My father stops and pulls out his wallet. I ask why he's always giving money away. Men and boys got to have a little walking-around money in their pockets, he tells me. "A little something to make 'em feel good about themselves, at least for a little while. Otherwise, they get to thinking what's the use of staying in school. Of working . . . doing the right thing."

I ask how much he gave the last man. He don't say. Then,

right before he gets in the truck, he tells me that every boy or man he gives a dollar to . . . a job to . . . spends a little time with . . . is a boy or man who gets maybe another day or hour or a lifetime to do right by himself and his family. "That's worth more than money, son."

CHAPTER 16

"YO, MALEEKA! YOUR chariot is here!" I stand up in Caleb's yellow convertible and bow. Girls across the street from Maleeka's house laugh right in my face.

Caleb tells me I won't get no dates to the prom this way. I climb into the back seat and tell him about Ashley. She stopped me in the hall. She ain't want nothing, I don't think. But she smiled at me a lot. "She's gonna be my girlfriend." If it had happened the other day, I woulda told Dad.

Caleb likes to give me advice about girls when he's only had one girlfriend ever: Maleeka. I let him know I don't need his advice. Not today anyhow. Ashley stopping me in the hall was a sign that she doesn't care what her mother thinks. That she'll sneak to be with me if she got to.

"What about Char?" Caleb gives Maleeka a double beep this time. "Didn't she say she was going with you to the junior prom?"

I sit down. Put my feet on the passenger-side headrest. "Char is like a sister. So, no. Plus, I wouldn't want your girlfriend knowing all of my business."

"I see what you mean."

Maleeka comes out the house smiling. After she opens the door to get in, the first thing she does is kisses him. Sniffing him, she tells him he smells good. I ask how she knows it wasn't me putting out those good smells.

"Because stink doesn't come in a spray can." Caleb's got jokes. When he's around her, he's got plenty. On his way out the parking space, he holds her hand.

Maleeka puts on lip gloss, checks out her lips in the mirror. Says she needs to get back home right after Caleb's dad's birthday party is over. "Me, Mom, and Mr. Porter are having a family meeting."

How they family, I ask, when he ain't married to her mom yet?

"He's a nice man," Maleeka says.

Caleb tells her he'll make sure she's home by six thirty. "My father goes to bed early and too many people tire him out."

I warn Maleeka that it's gonna be different with Mr. Porter in the house. "Everything gets messed up when you get a stepmother or stepfather. Your family isn't ever the same."

She don't agree. But girls watch a bunch of movies so they still believe in fairy tales. They think everything will work out okay because they want it to. But she'll see. One day it'll just happen. Her mom will choose his side more than hers. She won't even notice she's doing it. Dad never did. He picked his wife's nephew for his best man, after he said I'd be his best man. Sheila thought we both should do it because she is her nephew's godmother, and her son was too young. Mom and her argued so much, Dad decided not to have a best man.

Caleb changes the subject and brings up junior prom. He asks Maleeka who I should go with when I know he already knows what she thinks because they talk about everything. Maleeka says I need a plan B instead of only focusing on Ashley. Smiling, she says, "I can also see you going with somebody like—"

"Do not say Char."

"No. Char is too—"

"Old for me?"

"No."

"Tall?" Caleb's dying, laughing at his own joke.

She asks if I'd go by myself. She would if she didn't have Caleb. That's what she says anyhow.

"But you have me." At the light, he kisses her on the mouth. "I tell you we're going to the same college?" Caleb looks at me in the mirror.

I ask Maleeka if it's true. She don't say yes or no, just that she loves him and she always will. And she wants Char and me to find somebody to love too.

"I'm in love with myself." I kiss my arm. "I'm just looking for a girl who can appreciate all this good-looking chocolate."

Maleeka shakes her head. Caleb turns up the music. I ask Maleeka what she thinks about Caleb trying to work two jobs. The other day he put in five more applications. How I know he never mentioned it to her?

Maleeka's head turns so fast I'm surprised her neck don't break. "Two?"

"I'm only thinking about it."

She wants to know why he ain't tell her. Not that she gives him time to answer. It's a dumb idea, she thinks, only she says it nicer than that. "You're always tired. You don't even start your homework until after eleven sometimes. And when I text you, a lot of times you don't text back."

"I'm busy!"

I never heard him raise his voice at her before.

Now she's yelling. "Don't holler!"

"And quit worrying about me. Worry about your own mother."

Can't believe he said that. I ask Maleeka if she wants my dad to check her mother's fiancé out, to change the subject. "He knows everybody."

Soon as the car stops, she unbuckles her seat belt. "Just because your family is screwed up, John-John, and yours too, Caleb, it doesn't mean mine is gonna be."

CHAPTER 17

MALEEKA GIVES ME this *look* when I go to open Caleb's front door. I move out the way and let him go in first. "Why are the lights off?" he says. Right then they come on.

"Happy birthday, Caleb!" everyone says. Maleeka is the loudest.

People come from everywhere wishing him a happy birthday, blowing streamers and birthday horns. His father comes over to us in a wheelchair with his wife pushing. "We got him, Natalie. We got . . . him." He didn't feel much like celebrating his birthday this year, Mr. P. tells everyone. "But I wanted . . . Caleb to have . . . the . . . best . . . birthday ever . . . son."

Caleb's real birthday is in three weeks.

He hugs his father. "Love you, Dad."

"Love you more."

Caleb's grandmother comes out the kitchen carrying a three-layer cake with green candles. We all start singing. It gets wild after that. Loud and noisy. More cousins of his come into the house. More food. The music gets turned up. I can dance better than almost anybody. I start with Caleb's little cousins because they ask me. Lifting them up, I dance 'em around the room. Drinking soda in between, I move up to older ones. I get Caleb's mother next. She quits stirring potato salad in a bowl on the table to line dance with the rest of us. Maleeka is on my left. Caleb's on my right. Three songs later, they're in a corner. Close together.

Apologizing to each other probably.

I'm sweating when I go find Mr. P. "I can get you something to drink. More food." The paper plate in his lap got fish bones on it and runny tuna salad.

"Just . . . sit . . ."

I go to find a chair and drag it over. When Mr. P.'s eyes shut, I figure he's asleep. But he ain't, he says, after I stand up to get a drink. He's dancing inside, having fun, he says, like he wished he had all those times when his wife asked him to take her on a cruise or to somebody's anniversary party, and he stayed late to work or worked ten, twelve days in a row.

"I didn't know you liked to dance."

His eyes open. "Me either." They close again. "Not . . . until . . . I got . . . sick. Don't wait . . . until . . . bad things happen . . . to live your life . . . John."

Watching people dance, I think about what Mr. P. said the whole time I'm at his party. It's sort of what Mom said a lot after the divorce. She stayed home to take care of me when I was little. After I got in school, she worked for Dad. One day she woke up and wanted something different, she said. I think she wanted a different husband too. She's the one who brought divorce up first.

CHAPTER 18

MR. P. IS RIGHT. You gotta live your life. Who knows, I could get shot dead tonight and die without ever being kissed. So, last night when I got home, I made myself a promise. Three. I'm gonna ask Ashley to junior prom. And make her say yes. If she don't, I'll ask around school until somebody else does. If everybody says no—I'm transferring.

Ashley drives to school with her mother, so she's usually here before the rest of us. I see her over there now. I go to her before I can change my mind. She looks stunned when I pull a chair up to hers. "Hey, Ashley." If she could see my underarms, she'd know how nervous she got me.

"Shhh," she says, smiling.

I take off my backpack. Sit it in my lap and start taking out candy. "I bought it. For you," I whisper.

She don't eat coconut. That's what she says anyhow. I got mints. Gum. Tic Tac. Because I came ready. Only, I don't offer her nothing else. I look around to make sure nobody can see me, before I get down on one knee, then two. Admiring the shape and color of her eyes, I come out and say it. "Wanna go to the junior prom?" I clear my throat and look around again. "With me, I mean." I cough to clear my throat this time. "I won't do nothing disrespectful." I rub my neck because my voice is going. "You're . . . ahhh . . . the prettiest girl at this school. I'll pay for your ticket."

A boy near the stacks laughs. I ain't see him before. I get off my knees. Don't want no pictures out there.

Ashley rubs her hands together, like it's cold in here. "You're so nice, John."

Uh-oh.

Staring at the papers on the desk she says, "But, no thank you." She accidentally knocks over a bottle of water. It wets the library book and papers spread on the table. I run to get paper towels. That boy laughs louder this time. "You stupid?" I hear him say. "You must be stupid. Her mother won't let her go to the junior prom with none of us."

I slow down.

He ain't done yet. Following me, he says, "She already told me no."

I take a different way back to Ashley. Help her clean up. She takes my wet trash, adds it to hers, and walks 'em to the can across the room. "I never been to a dance. Or a party," she says, sitting back down.

"Never, ever?" I look at him, then back at her.

"Not in my whole life."

"I thought you were lying."

"It's okay. I don't miss 'em."

I know she's lying. Like I was lying when I used to say I didn't miss my father living with us. I whisper and promise if she goes with me, she won't ever forget junior prom for the rest of her life. "Because I will make sure you don't." I look down at the floor, then over at him. "It'll be the way I'll dance with you,

Ashley. The way I'll treat you, more special than you ever been treated before. The way I'll make you laugh and feel." The words keep coming. I don't even know where from. But a girl with eyes like hers. One as nice as she is. Well, she deserves a nice boy. Me. And I don't care what *he* thinks over there.

Ashley looks at me the way I been wanting a girl to look at me my whole life. After she says yes, I'm going over there to tell him. I'll call my father next and let him know I don't got to be like everybody else to get what I want.

"No."

I look at her like I didn't hear what I just heard. "No?"

"No."

That's not what you were supposed to say, I wanna tell her. I planned everything out last night. It was supposed to go different, even if her mother doesn't like boys like us. Because Ashley likes me. I know it.

He's over there holding his stomach, laughing.

Sometimes I can be like my father. "Okay." I stand up, frowning at her. "But you missed your chance." Dad can hurt your feelings. "And don't think I'll ask you anymore." And once he closes a door, Mom says, sometimes it's shut for good, forever, mostly because he said something so mean it makes the person on the other side want to keep it that way. "I could get a girl prettier than you any day of the week." It just comes out.

I'm walking away when something hard hits the back of my head. Her shoe.

CHAPTER 19

I GET TO book club before Ashley, Char, or Maleeka. Only me and Ariel are here. Good, she's who I need to see. I freshen my breath on my way over to her. "Yo, Ariel." I walk slow, cool. "You wanna go"—I swallow—"to junior prom with me?" I sit down beside her, too close, I think.

She blows a big pink bubble, then pops it with her teeth. "Nope."

I look down at my feet, thinking about the boy in the library spying on Ashley this morning. I'm lying when I tell Ariel that my father's got a new BMW that he said he'd let me drive to the junior prom. Really, he said if I got me a date he'd drive us in it.

"Double no."

Last night, I told my father I changed my mind about going. I said I had studying to do. "Books always gonna be there," he told me. "I didn't even finish my last year of high school or go to college. And look at me. I made two hundred thousand last year, after taxes."

I told him the junior prom didn't mean all that much to me, even though it do. He brought up Mr. Junior's sons and other boys who live in this neighborhood. "What's wrong with you, JJ?"

"Nothing."

"You ain't like I was when I was your age. Nothing like most boys that come to me for advice."

"Mom always said I didn't have to be like anybody else. That liking archery and playing checkers was okay," I told him.

"Well, I'm telling you it ain't!" He got real quiet for a while. "Find some different hobbies, for God's sake. You know what they say on the street to me? He your son? That boy? They shocked you don't play football. That you ain't beating down the backboard like I used to do in school."

I sit down in my usual book club seat, thinking maybe Dad is right. That maybe everybody is when it comes to me. What's the use of trying, then?

When Char comes in, I tell her this will be my last year being a part of book club. I joined to get a girlfriend. They all just wanna be my friend.

Out comes a licorice. Red. She brought them for her volunteer group, she tells me. "But you look so pitiful, I got to share 'em with you."

"Thanks." I open the pack. Take six. Open my book. In comes Ashley, late. Sitting across from me, she waves to Char. Ariel leans over and whispers in her ear. It's about me. I know it.

"Ignore 'em." Char crosses her legs. She turns to the chapter we're supposed to talk about. And tells me not to be so desperate. "It's just a dance. And sorry to say it, John-John, but sometimes we don't get what we want." Char looks at me. "I didn't want to get kicked out of my house and for all those bad things to happen to me. I ain't want my parents to die."

I didn't want my mother and father to divorce. But things

work out the way they should, she says. I look up at Ashley again.

"I think I blew it for good with her." I tell Char the whole story. "Guess her going to the junior prom with me ain't happening, huh?"

Char's got me by the hand when she says most likely I'm right. But she bets I'll go with somebody; a girl that I'll have as much fun with as Ashley.

"Yeah, right."

CHAPTER 20

I CAME TO the park to show Caleb why I'm his worst nightmare when it comes to archery. Plus, when I feel like this, I need to be out here sweating, shooting, pulling off my shirt, flexing my biceps, giving my chest muscles a workout.

If I had my stuff in school yesterday, I tell Caleb, they woulda been in that library dude's back. Don't joke about things like that, he says. "It could get you expelled."

I stop climbing the hill we're on. "Out here?"

"Just don't say things like that. It can get you in trouble, even if you're playing around. Anyhow, boys like us are different . . ."

I open my mouth to say something, but he keeps talking. "No matter what Ashley's mother thinks, they're not better than us."

"I just want a date."

I spray-paint a shooting line on the grass. He sets up the target near a tree. I'll go first. Putting on my shooting glove, I stretch, get into position, aim, release. And remember how good I am at this. I think about my father and his big mouth too. About that dude in the library again. I hit the target, bullseye every time. How come I don't get it 100 percent right with girls? When it comes to them, I'm Caleb, out here missing shots no matter how hard he tries.

After his turn, I collect arrows off the ground, out the tree and the target, wondering if Ashley woulda said yes to the dude who laughed at me if it weren't for her mother.

Caleb draws the bow back, fires. Jumps up when it gets closer than it ever did before. Walking over to me, he taps my fist with his. "I got an A on my test today too."

"About time."

We should be on our way home. Mom wants me to mow. Caleb's father called, said he needed something from the store. Neither one of us wants to leave. When we do, it's two hours later. Caleb's still smiling. In the car, he tells me his mother met with the bank. They said they thought they could work something out with them. *So y'all can keep the house*, I almost say. But if he wanted me to know, he'd tell me.

When I get home, my mother's not in the house. She's good for leaving notes though. She went door to door with a petition, it says. The city is picking up the trash too late on Fridays and she's the block captain. They need two hundred signatures, to make the city pay attention, it says. *Eat dinner without me. I'll be late.*

I eat with the dogs. Then go hide my equipment in the yard in the tree house Dad built for me. Mom almost found my bow in my room the other day. Dad and me both agree, she can't know I got it.

CHAPTER 21

"YOUR FATHER'S GONNA be mad." As soon as Mom opens the front door, she gets licked and jumped on. Me too. "I don't like it when you lie." Even in the dark I see their tails wagging.

Going in behind her, I close and lock the door. Let them lick my fingers, taste the hot dogs I ate, the soda that spilled all over my hand. "I didn't lie."

"You didn't cancel. You let your father come to the house knowing we weren't home. That is being dishonest."

I wanted to go to an archery competition two hours away. Mom got a friend to drive us. I told Mom the truth on the way home. She knew something was up, she says, because my phone kept ringing. It was Dad, only I never answered.

Mom starts turning on lights in the living room. Ends up in the kitchen with three dogs jumping on her. "Down, Mildred." Mom rubs and scratches her head.

I drag out the bag of dry dog food. The other dogs get something different, homemade food from Mom. They got no teeth. Just gums. I push them out the way and wash their bowls, using my fingers for a rag. I fill the bowls with food and sit on the floor in the kitchen with them. Mom asks about the yard.

I keep meaning to get to it. It's been two weeks since I mowed and forgot to bag the clippings. "Next week, Mom."

"And the dog poop?"

I knew she'd bring it up. With all these dogs, I could shovel my life away. She mentions the shovel by the front door. It's rusted. We use it for poop in the summer, snow in the winter. "I'll get a new one tomorrow," Mom says. "And I want everything taken care of by the end of the day."

I step over the gate on my way to the living room so I can go upstairs. Mom ends up blocking me. "So, should I get you a new suit for the junior prom? It's in four days."

"Why you and Dad keep asking me about that stupid prom?"

I don't mean to step on her foot. But I do. She's holding it, making faces after I apologize. I sit on the couch beside her. Massaging her foot, I ask if she knows how mean girls can be. When she was my age, she says, she reported a boy to the office.

Did he say something bad about her, I ask. She tells me no. Did he put her business out in the street, disrespect her? No, she says. "Then why you do it?

"He asked me to the prom."

"You went to the principal because you got asked to prom? Y'all girls make it hard on us, Mom."

He taped the note inviting her to the prom on the front of her locker, Mom says. A different boy was standing on a trash can reading it out loud by the time she got there. "He wouldn't give it to me when I asked." Mom's eyes blink and water like it's happening now. "He told me I was uglier than the boy who wrote the note."

Everybody in the hallway laughed. Then the boy who wrote the note said Mom might as well go to prom with her twin—the math teacher's Seeing Eye dog.

"After all this time"—Mom looks sad—"I still remember every word he wrote."

My mother gets stopped on the street all the time by other people who ask where she got her dress or shoes. Men stare at her a lot. If I saw that boy now, I'd smash his face in, I tell her.

She told on the boy who wrote the note, but not the one who stood on the can yapping. "I ain't want any more trouble."

I ask if Dad was the boy who invited her to the prom. Mom reminds me that they didn't meet until he was in his twenties. Then she tells me something I never knew. Dad paid a girl to go on a date with him once.

"How come you never told me?"

"It was a long time ago. Anyhow, your father said it never happened. But his friend's sister told me it did." She kisses my forehead. "Sometimes people who talk the loudest got the least amount of confidence, JJ."

"You mean Dad?"

Bending over to rub behind Malcolm's ear, Mom offers to go to the prom with me. I shake my head so hard it hurts. Hugging her, I think about my father and wonder what else he's lied to me about.

CHAPTER 22

MY STUFF GOT stolen. Somebody came into our yard and walked off with my bow and all my arrows, thirteen, even the case. It's that stupid light. It shines in our backyard too. Without it, they just came, went up in my tree house, and did whatever they wanted to. I had a baseball glove up there too. It's gone.

I can't sleep thinking about it.

Tired, mad, feeling stupid, I call Char. Around four o'clock, I just come out and ask her. What could she say, no, like all the other girls? I'm used to it anyhow.

"Char. Will you go to junior prom with me?"

"I said I would, didn't I?"

CHAPTER 23

DAD GAVE ME fifty dollars, said not to tell Mom. That some things are only between him and me, like my equipment being stolen, and me asking him about girls, like all the ones he swears he dated in high school.

"And don't lie, Dad. How many girlfriends did you really have?" I asked to find out how far behind him I am. I feel way behind, miles, even though junior prom is in a couple hours. But from what Mom said, maybe him and me would be even if we were the same age. Which means he should quit asking me about stuff.

"Let's just say . . . you got a lot of catching up to do, JJ." He went downstairs. Told Mom he'd wait for us outside.

I went and took a shower.

Getting out the car, I thank Char for the third time tonight for going to junior prom with me. My father hears me and shakes his head. Mom says, "Not one more word out of you, Big John. Not. One. Word. And y'all two have a good time."

Far as I can tell, Char's the only one dressed in a gown. She needed one for the dinner where she volunteers. And it didn't make sense to wear it just once, she told us. "Plus, they say you should dress the way you wanna be when you become an adult.

I wanna be special. Important. Somebody people write about in books," she told Mom.

Soon as we're out the car, Mom starts with the pictures again. I kiss her cheek and don't care who sees. Char doesn't care that Mom just kissed her cheek either. "Your parents would be proud of you," Mom tells her.

My father leans against his new ride. Dressed in all white, except for the black ring around his hat, he crosses his legs. Kids stare at him. They check out his ride. I hear somebody say how nice it is. It's a black BMW SUV with tinted black windows and tires that have so much chrome you could see 'em from space.

"Yo, Big John." Some man walks up to him. Their hands dance. He points to a boy and girl taking pictures on the steps. "That's my son."

I don't hear everything, but I do hear him ask Dad if he could find a job for his boy this summer.

"You kidding. Yeah." My father looks over at me. "Can't wait for JJ to work for me. But you know how kids are. They think working for someone else is better than working for the person who puts food on the table."

Mom clears her throat.

Char, me, and a whole bunch of other kids start up the steps. We stop to take more pictures. Floodlights shine on the building, grass, and trees, turning everything yellow, orange, red, or light green. A girl dressed in silver spins around twice. "I won't ever forget tonight, not ever," she tells the boy who came with her.

Char smiles. "Me either." Her arm goes through mine. Music

hits us right when the doors open. Stopping, Char asks how she looks.

"Beautiful." I mean it too.

Her dress is a soft blue. Those are Char's words, not mine. Her shoes sparkle. And she's got on a crown. Her sister, JuJu, had it made in New York. Holding on to it like it might fall off, Char says, "I had to wear it, didn't I?"

"Yeah, Char." I'm real close to her when I stare in her eyes. "You and me. We gonna have fun." I hug her because she helped me get here. And being here is gonna help me get to the next dance and the next dance and the senior prom—maybe even with Ashley. 'Cause girls see you with other girls at something like this, and they want you. That's just how it is, my father said while I was getting dressed.

"Char."

"Yeah."

"This ain't no pity date, is it?"

"It's just a dance, John-John."

CHAPTER 24

MISS SAUNDERS IS like air. She be everywhere. Soon as we get in the building, we see her on the podium, at the microphone talking over the music. "We will separate you if you're too close to your partner. So, please don't make us." She waves at some of the kids, calling us by name, saying how nice we look.

Maleeka comes out of nowhere wearing a plum-colored dress—Char calls it that anyhow. It's short. Tight. I gotta try hard not to look at her legs. "Caleb better watch out," I say, wondering where he's at.

The glass ball hanging from the ceiling spins, sending silver dots flying everywhere, touching everything: the walls and floor, our clothes, teachers dressed like they still in class, drinks and food on tables.

People already dancing. It's mostly girls with girls. Boys stand by the wall talking, pointing at people, laughing. I gave that up in middle school. But I know how it goes. Everybody wants to take you down. Catch you dropping the ball. "How my breath smell, Char?" I blow in her face.

"Why you do that?" Her fingers turn into a fan. "And how you think it's gone smell? You had garlic wings at the house."

Maleeka opens a purple purse the size of my palm. "Here."

She shakes mints into my mouth. "I already had some." Taking me and Char by the arm, she goes to the middle of the floor. Before I know it, we out there dancing. Caleb too once he shows up. They got dropped off separately. He went to pick up his new pants and a shirt, but the store where he bought 'em was closed. His uncle had to drive him around to find something else to wear. By the time Caleb got home, showered, and spent time with his dad, he was running late. He told Maleeka to meet him here. She don't seem mad.

In a little while, there's so many people on the floor it's hard to move. I pop another mint. Lean in close. "Let me know when you get tired, Char."

"I ain't gone get tired." She turns and her dress floats out like a sheet. Stopping, she whispers in my ear. It's about Ashley. I can't hear all of it. So, Char turns me around and points to Ashley, who's on the opposite side of the room. She's all by herself, looking prettier than I ever seen her. More beautiful than Char and Maleeka put together.

"I thought she wasn't allowed to come?" I say.

Char don't say nothing. Maleeka tells me I better go talk to her now, while I can.

"I wasn't so nice to her the last time."

"Apologize." They say it at the same time.

"But what if she—"

Maleeka points to him, the boy from the library. "Better not let him get to her first."

CHAPTER 25

I AIN'T LEAVE the building because I'm scared of him. I want to think about what I'll say to Ashley, that's all.

Across the street, away from everyone, I rehearse. "Ashley, will you dance with me?" I say in my head.

"No." I say it because she might. Girls can hold grudges.

Caleb finds me on the sidewalk, near the bushes, sweating and thinking. He don't say a word. Not for a while anyhow. "Would you?" is all I say.

"If I liked her a lot."

I wipe sweat from behind my ears. "What if he likes her too?"

"You know how many boys like Maleeka?"

"Yeah, everyone in this school."

"But she loves me." Caleb smiles. "And I love her. I can't worry about other people." He asks if I'm ready to go in. Without waiting, he crosses the street, starts up the steps to our school. But he don't go inside until I catch up. I tell him that I know how I look, almost running out the building. Sweating a girl who might spit on me. "Thanks." He knows what I mean.

He says it ain't nothing, but it is. You can't let your boys see you looking weak, especially over no girl 'cause some dudes run and tell everything. It can help their reputation, depending on what they're telling. And make them feel important. A real friend keeps secret what you want secret, like what Caleb tells me right before we go in. He's decided not to return to school in September. There's too much to do at his house. "And the bank called." He looks around to see who might hear. "They turned my parents down."

CHAPTER 26

I ALWAYS LOSE. He got to Ashley before I did. I can't tell if she wants him there or not. He's blocking my view of her. But he don't stay long. Maybe she don't want neither one of us. Maybe she ain't interested in me or him, I tell Caleb.

"You won't know unless you go find out," he says, walking up to Maleeka. Taking her hand.

I find Ashley near the steps you take to get onstage. She's got a program in her hand, rolled up, twisting it tight when I get to her. My hands stay in my pockets. "Hey, Ashley."

She's looking at the floor, not me.

You look nice, smell good. Wish I could say that. It's the decorations I talk about. I joke about Miss Saunders too. How she should be a cop the way she following people around, getting in between 'em when they dance. Ashley don't say nothing. Finally, I come out and apologize.

I still get nothing.

I let her know I saw him with her a little while ago. "Did you want me to leave too?"

"No!"

"He likes you, I think."

"Well, I don't like him."

I follow him with my eyes. "Ashley."

"Yeah, John."

"I'm glad you came." I take my hand out my pocket. Reach for hers hoping she don't slap it; happy she doesn't.

"I wasn't told I could come until yesterday. My aunts spoke with my mom about it. They bought my dress. And paid to get my hair done." She pats her long, wavy hair. "They told my parents if they didn't want me to sneak around, they needed to give me some breathing room. So, this is a test." She scratches the tip of her nose. "My mother said it. If I go against her rules"—she lets my hand go—"I can't if I want her to trust me with more responsibility." Ashley looks up at me for the first time. "But I'm glad I'm here, John. I really am."

I start talking about stupid stuff, like book club. I got to. Otherwise, I might say what I'm thinking, what I'm feeling. "We only meet two more times." I swallow.

Ashley gets a big smile on her face. "I'll miss it."

"Me. Too." I take her hand back, rubbing it with my thumb. I come out and ask her what I'm thinking. "Will you miss me over the summer?"

"A lot."

"Maybe I should leave, huh?" I say it because I'd be hurt if she took away what she just said to me.

Her eyes and mine don't look nowhere else but at each other's. I try to memorize the shape of her lips. How warm her fingers are. The way she smells—sweet as the flowers in the yard behind ours.

Next thing I know, here come Maleeka in a hurry, ruining our good time. "Ashley!" It's hard for her to catch her breath.

"Your . . . your . . . mother. Wants you. Now. That's exactly what she said."

Ashley don't waste no time getting away from me. But she can't get away from her mother. In the middle of the room, her mom catches up to her. Hollers at her. I can't hear all of what her mother says because of the music. Ashley does though. I see it on her face. And by the way she's standing there—like a tree is about to fall on her.

CHAPTER 27

I RUN UP the steps to Caleb's house. Their door stays unlocked most times, so I walk in hollering, "Hey, Caleb! Caleb!"

He got an attitude I see. "I'm giving my father a bath. How come you don't know that? Every Saturday, same time." The bathroom door slams shut.

I know. I just forgot. Maybe because I got her on my mind. Last Saturday was the best night of my life.

I couldn't do it though, wash my father up. Powder his feet and private parts. Help him put on clean underwear. But at least Caleb don't have to do it every day. Only once a week. His mom and his father's brothers shower him the other times. Caleb's mother says he doesn't need to do it at all. That he needs to get out the house more, enjoy being a teenager. He wants to, Caleb says. "I love my father. He would do anything for me."

In the kitchen, I find a peach in the refrigerator waiting on me. I eat it. Get another one and throw the pits in the trash can by the sink. I feel bad about what I just did.

I'm in the living room, putting pieces in a puzzle on the coffee table, when I hear Mr. P. shuffling around upstairs in the hallway. He moves like he don't trust his feet to get him where he needs to go. On walks, he holds on to both our arms. Before the aneurysm, he jogged, golfed on weekends, ran their cleaning business. Mr. P. was doing the accounting, bringing in new business, and still cleaning office buildings. His wife and his brothers were partners. They were better at cleaning than running the business, Caleb told me.

We're outside when I tell Mr. P. how cool he looks. I like it when he smiles. For a while he couldn't. Maybe he ain't want to. One side of his mouth drooped. His eyes watered. It was hard to use his right arm. He walked like a zombie. My father is right about one thing. You can't give up. Can't let people around you give up either. A therapist worked with Mr. P. at the house before their insurance company stopped paying. So did Caleb and his family. Now his father is a whole lot better, only he's still way different than before.

Caleb looks tired and it ain't even eleven o'clock. "Hold my arm, Dad." He sticks out his elbow. "Would you like a sweater?"

It's not cold, but sometimes Mr. P. gets a chill even when me and Caleb are hot and sweaty. "I think he does," I say.

"What do you think, Dad?" No matter how long it takes for his father to answer, Caleb will wait.

"A man stops feeling like a man and he's done for." My father said that once right in front of Caleb. We were talking about Mr. P. They ain't have a wheelchair ramp at the house then so he was stuck inside or on the porch day and night. My father built him one. He ain't ask for money or permission. He was being neighborly, he told Caleb's mother. He got permits and everything.

"The . . . green . . . one."

That's how it goes. Sometimes, you forget about the question by the time Mr. P. answers. "A whole day's done gone by and you're just picking out a sweater, Mr. P.?" Snapping my fingers, I let him know he's gotta think faster if he's gonna be around me. Caleb's uncle heard me say something like that once and went off on me. Mr. P. took my side. I'm the only one that treats him like he ain't sick, he told his brother. "So . . . stay out of our business!"

That surprised me because Mr. P. is a gentleman. He always said the right words at the right time. But, even like this, he's one of the best people I know.

Caleb and me take our time walking with him down the front porch steps. I keep my eyes on his feet. Can't have him tripping and falling. Caleb asks which direction he wants to go today? How many blocks he thinks he can walk? How long he wants to stay out? He doesn't want him to feel like no baby or invalid. He lets him make as many decisions as he can. I would probably just say, let's go this way.

Mr. P. used to walk so slow I'd end up daydreaming, thinking about something else, girls mainly, kissing 'em mostly. Now we be joking with him, me anyhow. Sometimes we get serious and talk about voting and racism, bad teachers, school shootings. I like talking to him about my father. Mostly, when it's only Mr. P. and me around.

Caleb's way behind us when I tell his dad I met a girl. Mr. P.'s left eye winks. "Tell me . . . about her." His smile is as crooked as a crack on the sidewalk. When I bring up Ashley's mom, he shakes his head and says maybe I should think about another girl. "This one . . . might . . . bring . . . you trouble."

"How? I don't even have her number."

If her mother doesn't think I'm good enough, eventually

Ashley may have doubts too, he thinks. "And a boy . . . has . . . as . . . much . . . right to feel good . . . proud . . . about . . . about . . . about himself as a girl does."

I like how he put that.

He needed some reminding too when he was my age, Mr. P. tells me. Because he didn't mature at the same rate as everyone else, he says. "Like . . . you."

"Why people think I'm not mature enough?" I rub the hairs I wish I had on my chin. I shaved this morning because I read somewhere you can make 'em come in faster that way. "Look what a good job I do taking care of Mom." I find a stone. Kick it in the street. "I bag the trash, watch stupid Hallmark movies with her, help cook and clean. Some dude came to our house, and I had to chase him off with the shovel for bad-mouthing Mom. And that's the truth."

Me and Caleb are good sons, Mr. P. says. Reaching up, he touches my right shoulder, squeezing it. "If anything happens to me . . ."

"Nothing's gonna happen to you, Mr. P."

"If it does—"

I ain't listening, I tell him. That if something happens to him, God is gonna have a problem with me. He asks me about Caleb next. How he's doing. "Fine," I say.

"The truth, John."

"He's good."

"That's what my son . . . says. But . . . it's . . . not the truth." He squeezes my arm. "This thing . . . is . . . changing . . . everybody, including . . . me. I don't . . . recognize myself . . . anymore."

CHAPTER 28

WE ON THE porch when Caleb takes his father's glasses off. Mr. P.'s eyes close right away. Next thing we know, he's snoring. Caleb's sitting across from me near the railing. I'm closer to his father. I been waiting all this time to talk to Caleb about Ashley, so I stand up and lean against the railing. I need some advice about her.

Before I get my thoughts out, Caleb brings up his dad. He wants to know if I think Mr. P. is getting better, because Caleb does. I lie and tell him what he wants to hear. His dad is better. He'll be back at work before we know it, I say. Then I go in the house, get gloves and a baseball out the vestibule. In the middle of the street, we talk and play catch. Caleb brings up my father.

"I owe him," he says.

I start to throw the ball, then stop. "You don't owe him nothing."

Caleb says he was at the grocery store last night. In line with his wallet out. He could see he was gonna be short. He was deciding what not to buy when my father popped up. "I didn't know he was in the store."

"It's gonna come out your pay." I throw the ball over his head accidentally. It rolls under an SUV. I didn't think he would go get it. Coming back, brushing off his pants, Caleb says his mom works seven days a week now. "That's another reason why I need to quit school."

"Don't tell her that."

He throws me the ball. "You really don't need college."

I throw the ball hard as I can. Caleb catches it, takes off the glove, shaking his hand. "At school . . . I make straight As without studying."

"You used to, you mean."

"I probably could pass—"

"Don't say it."

"—the GED in my sleep."

I walk up to him. "What?"

"I've been thinking, that's all."

"Well, stop. Anyhow, you can't drop out. We're this close to graduating." I put my fingers together like when Mom takes a pinch of salt. "Like you said, you can do high school in your sleep. So do it. But don't drop out. That's stupid."

His relatives help out, he says. But sometimes they complain. The other day, he heard his father's brothers on the front porch talking about how hard all this was on everybody. One of them said maybe his dad should be in a nursing home.

I look at his father. "Not Mr. P." Then I whisper, "Y'all can't do that to him."

"You see now why I need the money?"

I see.

Plus there's medicine to pay for, he says. Physical therapists. A special bed upstairs they pay for by the month. "Plus our house might get—never mind." Caleb walks up to me, throwing the ball from his glove to his hand. "I have to work, that's all I know. School won't pay your bills."

Caleb had his own business, moving lawns. Two summers in a row. When his father got sick, Caleb had four thousand dollars in the bank. Plus, his parents still gave him an allowance and paid for his gas. They wanted him to use the money for college. He's down to zero. His family ain't got much more than that.

For like twenty minutes, we go at it, not talking, just throwing. The sun is hotter than when we first came out. So my whole shirt ends up soaked. My scalp too. Caleb looks tired, like he wanna take a nap. "You good?" I ask.

"I'm good." He stops, takes off his glove to crack his knuckles. "Life sucks."

"I told you it did."

"Well—you lie sometimes."

Yeah, I do. But not about life. Even at our age it knocks you down, bullies you worse than Char ever could. But you got to get back up every time, all the time, I tell him. "Otherwise, it will stomp you in the face and laugh at you."

"That's funny." He leans against the SUV. "Are you hot? I'm hot." He wipes away sweat, holds his head with both hands. "And my head hurts."

"Want some water?"

He sits on the ground. Pulls off the glove and lies down next, like the ground is a bed. "Just give me a minute." Caleb says he feels like he might faint or throw up at the same time.

I think about his father's aneurysm. Ask if he wants me to call the police, an ambulance. "'Cause this is what you said your father told you when he—"

"I'm thirsty. I just need water."

I go to the house. Come back with a glass of ice-cold water and some candy. Caleb's still on the ground. Mr. P. is still asleep.

"Here. Sit up."

He don't move. I sit down beside him. "Let me help you up." My arm's shaking, the water is jumping around in the glass. So I sit everything on the ground. Do what I need to do to get him sitting up. "Drink it." I got to hold the glass when he does, 'cause he's so weak. Pouring water in my hand, I rub it over his forehead, down his arms. "Here, eat a mint. Maybe you're hungry. You eat today?" I open my hands. "Could be your sugar is low. My cousin's a diabetic, type two. Mints help sometimes."

"I'm not a diabetic." He drinks a little more before he takes the mint from me.

"Take two more. And don't say you ain't hungry. Did you eat?" I look at the neighbors in the windows looking at us.

The mints melt in your mouth. But he chews 'em. Washes 'em down with more water. "Got any more?"

I leave and come back with a peach.

"Maybe I was . . . hungry," he says, taking a bite.

I ask him again what he ate today.

"An egg."

"That's it."

"I had stuff to do."

I sound like my mother, yelling at him about getting sick because he ain't taking care of hisself. "I'm good," he says, trying to get up.

"No, you ain't. Stop lying." I stand up. Reach down. But he don't accept my help. It takes him a while to get to the steps, onto the porch, into the house. In the living room, he sits on the first chair he gets to. I don't think he could go no farther.

"Could you go to the kitchen and—"

"I got you."

I make him a peanut butter and jelly sandwich. Bring back applesauce, ice cream, just in case. He eats everything on his plate.

CHAPTER 29

CALEB WAS HAVING a bad day when he picked me up. Me too. I had to clean the whole house with Mom. One room, top to bottom, every day this week. I don't know what his problem is.

A little while ago he shot a arrow, hit a tree, broke the tip. Twice. I ain't mean to shove him, but I did. Told him he was getting on my nerves too. I wanna talk about girls, not bills. Come to the park to shoot archery, not hear him talk about how many loads of laundry he did this week.

You always been selfish, he said, pushing me. I push him so hard he falls down. Didn't stay down though. When he got up, I ran up behind him, jumped on his back. Took him down again. It was crazy. Maybe it was too hot. Maybe we were just tired. His dad had a bad night, I found out. Didn't sleep good. His mother wasn't there, she was at work. Which means Caleb was up all night with his father, so he skipped school today, came to my house a couple hours ago with bags under his eyes and an attitude. I got my own problems, I told him. "Mom took away my allowance for the month 'cause she doesn't like how I did the yard." I'm not no maid, I told Mom. "How much work around here you want me to do?"

What I say that for? Spring cleaning is both our jobs, she told me. Then she added the part about losing my allowance. So, I didn't wanna hear Caleb complaining. I just didn't. By the time we left, we were cool. Like I say, we like brothers, we don't hold grudges.

—

CHAPTER 30

I DON'T COME out and say it the next day. I hint around to Dad about Caleb and me fighting. I ought to get into more fights anyhow, he tells me. "Both of you should." He reaches over and squeezes my arm muscles. Says he's got some weights he ain't using.

"I'm good."

"It's rough out here, JJ. Y'all two better learn how to fight if you plan to make it in life."

You don't need to know how to fight to have your own television network or make movies, I tell him.

"Who told you that?" He pushes his plate to the side and waves the waitress over. "Businessmen might not use fights, but they will pulverize you in some rooms, beat you till you crying for your momma if you can't defend yourself during negotiations or when you trying to close on a loan or keep the city from swallowing up your whole neighborhood so other people can buy it dirt cheap."

"I'm good at talking. I can do that."

The waitress pours more black coffee in his cup. And leaves six packs of sugar. Dad blows the steam and makes too much noise when he sips. "You good? Need anything?"

"I'm good."

My father sits a twenty on the table. "A man always needs money."

I take it, put it away quick. With what's in my drawer, this will give me seventy dollars toward a new bow and some arrows.

The waitress clears the table. Dad brings up one of his friend's sons. They went to a party last week, he tells me. Got home three in the morning. I didn't expect him to say that's a little late for somebody our age. He asks what my curfew is.

"Mom says next year it'll change. She ain't told me what it'll be yet. Right now . . . be in the house at ten on weeknights, she says. Eleven on weekends if I got something to do. Like a party or a movie to go to. But I gotta let her know ahead of time."

His eyes roll. He shakes his head. I don't like it either, I tell him. But it is what it is.

What do I think it should be, he asks. "Midnight on Saturdays, for sure," Dad tells me.

If I was another boy, he says, he would suggest a later time. "Only, you not like other boys. You ain't no fighter. We all know that. And in these streets, you got to be able to protect yourself."

Here we go again. Don't even know I ain't listening. I'm listening to her now. Ashley. She's telling me how much she misses seeing me in school. I tell her I been avoiding her. They say her mother ain't been so nice to boys who need to come to the office. That the principal had a conversation with her about it. In the hall, at book club, Ashley don't even look at me. But it's like our hearts beat at the same time. How I tell my father that? He over here talking about Muhammad Ali and other boxers who I ought to be watching on television "instead of gladiators and knuckleheads like them. You paying attention, boy?"

"Huh?"

He brings up Mr. Charles's son. He's taking boxing lessons at Jim's Gym on Tenth, six blocks from here. "Let's go check the place out. You might like it."

"I'm cool." I finish my iced tea.

Dad says we can maybe go on Saturday, bring Caleb and have us a nice lunch in the Chamber of Commerce building downtown afterward. He starts throwing hands. "You two could pick up a few tips from Eric, maybe get into the ring." My father acts like he's in the ring, ducking, throwing punches at me, forcing me to duck too.

"Quit it!"

"That boy's going to the Olympics one day." He reaches for his coffee.

"Does anybody care, Dad?"

"You ought to. He could teach you some things."

I take out the money he gave me and sit it on the table. "You don't know what I know or don't know." I leave the table.

He jumps up. "Where you going? Get back here."

I get back to the table so quick, you'd think I flew. "We was having a good time! You ruined it. Why you always do that?!"

I need to quit being so sensitive, Dad says, not caring that people are staring. And quit wearing my feelings on my sleeve. "In this world it'll hurt you way more than it'll help you, boy."

I step around a waitress. "And don't call me boy. I hate that."

He takes out his wallet. Throws her tip on the table. I start walking away again.

"Did you hear me? Get back here, boy!"

He's always loud. Always got to be heard. Got to be seen. Everybody in here's watching us. Outside, moving like I got wheels for feet, I pass his black BMW, a store we stopped in earlier, the laundromat Mom takes oversized blankets to. I only stop walking when a police car drives over the sidewalk right in front of me on its way to the station. There's a boy in back. Him and me the same color. Could be the same height, same age. His hands are behind his back, handcuffed. Tears run down his cheeks. We look at each other. Look away just as quick.

"These streets can't have you, JJ." Mom says it a lot. "And I won't help 'em take you from me either."

Did his mother ever say that to him? Do she know where he's at? Mom would cry a ocean if I ended up like him.

My father pulls up beside me right when they take that boy out the car. His window rolls down, his lock pops open. "Get in, boy."

I do what he says. No questions asked.

We don't talk on the way home. The radio ain't on either. Maybe he's thinking about that boy. About me turning out like him 'cause like Mom says, it ain't always the bad ones that end up in the back of police cars.

CHAPTER 31

I GET OUT Dad's ride in front our house before his truck stops good.

"Got something for you in the trunk," he hollers.

I keep it moving.

"JJ, you hear me!"

"I ain't no kid." I smack my chest. "You want respect. I want some too."

His trunk opens. "So, you don't want this?"

I know I should go in the house, but I don't. I watch him get out the car. Leave the door open. Go to the trunk. I almost can't breathe when I see what's in his hand. It would take me six more months to save enough money to buy it.

"Sweet—" Not that it makes up for how he treated me in the restaurant. But I need it. I feel . . . like I can do anything when I'm holding it. I just might enter a competition one day. "Thanks, Dad. I mean it. Thanks." Before he can say it, I do. "Don't tell Mom."

We're still by his car when Dad brings up the times me and him used to watch a movie about a girl who used a bow and arrows to hunt people and food. It's in a case. I put it over my shoulder. I saw that movie so many times I knew all of her lines. Still do. He got to thinking about the one that was stolen. "Thinking about a lot of things," he says. "Maybe me and you can do it together. Go hunting or something."

"It's illegal to kill animals with a bow and arrow."

He digs his hands in his pockets. When he does that, I know a speech is coming. Maybe an apology. I tell him never mind. I'm tired. He don't listen to me.

"One day you'll understand. Men do the best they can. My father was hard on me too."

Just back up, sometimes, I wanna say. *Let me figure things out for myself.* It's on the tip of my tongue. *If I mess up, I mess up. If I lose a fight, it's on me. Just stop acting like I'm a little kid . . . 'cause I ain't. I'm almost a man, no matter what you see.* It's all right there in my head. But he interrupts me like always. Almost makes sense this time too. I can't beat my father at talking or nothing else.

He never liked to follow the rules, he says. He ran away in middle school. Almost got locked up a time or two. That won't ever be me, he knows it, he tells me. "But if it ever is you . . ." He needs to know I can handle myself, he says, not looking at me. Then out of nowhere he says, "I'm old, boy. I won't always be around, you know."

I look at his eyes, watering. "I know, Dad."

On the way to the car, I can see my father's knee is bothering him. I didn't notice it at the restaurant. I did see his hands, fingers. He's got arthritis in his knuckles. They the size of prunes. He soaks 'em at night when they ache too much, he told me once. "My business is hard on the body," he said that day. "I'm paying for it now."

CHAPTER 32

IS HE IN the library because of Ashley or is he like me, hiding out? I got here early because of what happened with me and my father on Saturday. It got me to thinking. I better man up when it comes to Ashley. Stop acting like I'm scared of her mom. What girl wants a boy like that? Then I get here early to see her, and he's here. On purpose, I walk in his direction. Pass his table. Feel my baby finger jumping. I let out a deep breath when I get to her table.

Pulling a chair up, I feel like I won. "Hi." I look at her, then at him.

"Hi."

Already, I run out of words. "Um . . . we only got one more time to meet," I say, swallowing hard. "I mean book club . . . not us." It's not what I wanted to say, but it's something.

"I'll miss you." That's what I hear. Playing it back, I see I was wrong. "I'll miss it." Those are the real words. But I'm in book club. Maybe she'll miss me too.

Ashley pulls out a book. A pencil too. Next thing I know she's reading, underlining a lot.

"Um . . . It's hot in here, ain't it?" I pull at my shirt collar, clear my throat. Stare at him staring at us.

Her fingers look like wings, fanning her cheeks. "It is."

I'm out of words. "Well . . . I just came to say hi." For some reason, I feel shorter. Scratching my head, even though it don't itch, I ask if she's going to book club today. I answer the question my own self. "You always come."

"Yeah. I do always come." She whispers, "I like a boy who likes books and the library."

"I don't be reading 'em though. I listen."

"That's reading."

"And I come to the library because—" Because I ain't wanna get beat up at my last school and I'm just used to coming. That's the truth, but I keep it to myself. "Um . . . because I like to stay ahead in my work."

She gets all happy. "Me too!" Before I know it, she's got her backpack on the desk, composition books out, twelve. Math homework is done with regular lead pencils. In the corner of some pages she draws rainbows, and hairstyles not attached to heads.

"Nice." I'm not sure why she shows 'em to me.

"I really want to be an illustrator when I'm an adult."

"I thought—"

"I want to be a weatherperson too. I love science and math. I can illustrate children's books about the weather and go to schools and talk to them about it." Her mother wants her to be a college professor.

"She tell you what to wear too?"

I can tell I embarrassed her. So I change the subject. "My father is sort of like your mom. He wants me to be what he wants me to be. That ain't happening."

It's like she sees me for the first time. Ten minutes later, we still talking about dumb, stupid things parents do.

"Maybe I should leave." I say it, but maybe she's thinking it.

Her pencil rolls off the desk, onto the floor. We almost bump heads picking it up. "Here." I give it to her.

"Thanks."

Her eyes and mine don't look nowhere else but at each other's for a while. I'm trying to memorize everything about her, like her favorite color, orange. She wears it in different shades every day. I look at her bracelet, small, matching her earrings; they have diamonds in 'em, little ones. Maybe she's only got one pair, one bracelet. I never see her wear anything else. Even her shoes hardly change, but she ain't poor. They live in the suburbs, in a complex with gates. Once school's out, we won't see each other for a long, long while, I say.

She's quiet. Me too, now. I sit back. Look around the library. Think about him over there, wonder if he knows he don't stand a chance with Ashley. When a girl sits at his table, I almost laugh. He puts his hand over hers. Already done replaced Ashley, I see.

Ashley leans my way. "I had to tell him that I didn't like him and if he kept following me I'd tell the principal."

I ask if she did that for me. Right then, somebody bangs on the glass window, loud enough to make Ashley jump. It's Maleeka. "Ashley!" She comes in breathing hard, trying to catch her breath when she says, "Your . . . mother . . ." She sits down across from Ashley. ". . . wants you."

"You working for her now, Maleeka?" I ask.

She came in the building early to get a letter of

recommendation from the librarian, she says. When she walked up the hall, Ashley's mom asked if she knew where she was. "I got the internship." She's feeling herself, I can tell. "See, you were wrong about Mr. Porter."

Ashley packs up. "Thanks again." She holds up her pencil. "Sorry about my mother."

"You don't have to apologize."

"Yes, I do."

She's gone when Maleeka pinches my cheek. "John-John has a girlfriend."

"No I don't."

"You could. She likes you."

"You think?"

"Yeah. She doesn't mind getting into trouble with her mother over you."

I sit on the desk. Swing my feet. Stare at Ashley going up the hall. *Don't do nothing stupid*, I tell myself.

CHAPTER 33

IT'S THE LAST day of school, finally. Noise, trash, and kids everywhere. It just worked out with me sitting outside the building next to Maleeka.

"You okay?" I lean forward after I see the look on her face. Maleeka doesn't answer when I ask what's wrong. I always think it might be her mother.

Last week, she had three interviews in one day at the newspaper, Maleeka says. The internship came down to her and a boy our age. "The secretary told me I had it"—she can't stop blinking—"then she called and said I didn't have it. My mother's fiancé heard they gave it to a boy and now they're paying him." She whispers, "They wanted me to volunteer."

I ask if Caleb knows.

"No."

Thinking on it some, I say, "Dude talked them into it, I guess. You shoulda spoke up for yourself." I get punched for that.

She's got better grades than him, she says. More volunteer experience.

"How you know?"

"You think I should write a letter . . . to the editor?"

I shake my head no. Tell her it's probably not even worth it. Her phone rings. It's what's-his-name—her mother's fiancé.

He's running late. School buses are everywhere, I hear him say, so he wants her to meet him a couple blocks from here. "Outside the coffee shop."

When Maleeka starts walking, I start walking. "Don't tell Caleb," she says.

"Don't tell him your mother's fiancé is picking you up?"

"About the internship."

She don't want him to worry.

Why is everybody always telling me their secrets? "I won't. But you ever think that maybe dude needed the job more than you?" I'm thinking about Caleb when I say it.

She rolls her eyes.

Why girls always do that? Anyhow, what I said could be true. Plus, girls get everything. The head of our student council is a girl, so is our class president and the head of the photography club and the newspaper. They in charge of almost everything at school. Boys need to get some things too once in a while, I tell her. Then I step into the street.

She starts giving me a speech when she says the girls were at the school first. "It was only us until this year when they started accepting boys. Anyhow, I'm smarter than he is."

What if that boy's got problems at home, like Caleb? I say. And he needs the money worse than her. It could happen.

She looks even sadder, but still don't take his side. "Then I'm sorry for him. And I feel sorry for Caleb . . . all the time. But my therapist says it's okay to look out for myself too. To want good things to happen for me, especially if I've worked hard for them. I ain't do it in seventh grade. But now I do. I got to."

CHAPTER 34

NOW THAT I'M out of school, Mom got lists of things for me to do taped around the house. Walk the dogs three times a day, one says. Go to the grocery store for hamburger, gravy—it's something on the list like that every couple of days. Clean the stove and refrigerator; don't forget the microwave. I think she's punishing me because I don't have a job. School's only been out two weeks.

All morning, I ignored her calls. Now I'm out the house, on my way to meet Char. What else do I got to do? Maleeka's pouting at home about Caleb and the job. Caleb's working every day, seems like. I saw him mowing somebody's lawn on Saturday. Dad said he saw him someplace else, cutting bushes. I ain't interested in none of that.

In a couple of weeks Char will be in Alabama for the summer with her grandparents. She sounded nervous about it yesterday. I told her I'd come by and walk her home from work. Make her laugh 'cause I'm good at that.

Soon as I get there, she walks down the steps and over to me, pointing. "What is that?"

I came carrying. Got my new archery set in the case, strapped over my shoulder. On my way here, I stopped in the park and practiced. We keep it at Caleb's house now. In the shed.

Nobody will find it there. I tell Char I might have to use it to protect her.

I ain't surprised when she tells me to grow up.

We pass a graveyard. Walk up a few blocks a girl shouldn't be on by herself. "Don't nothing scare me," she says, after I mention it. This dude named Anthony scared her. But he's gone for good now, locked up. Anyhow, I got her back. Whenever she hears me say that, she laughs, then tells me that she can fight way better than me any day of the week. Most likely she's right. But if I'm anywhere near Char, I'm gonna look out for her. Maleeka too. I'll probably get stomped like a bug, but that's how it goes sometimes. Plus, once Char came back from running away, I knew she needed somebody. So, I'm her somebody now. I owe it to her, I think.

I'm kidding when I tell Char she needs to be paying me to walk her home. Only, she don't take it that way. "You ain't got to." Next thing I know, she's way up the block.

I run. Keep my mouth shut once I catch up to her. Until some man in a old, raggedy car beeps. I put my arm over her shoulder, tell her to ignore him. By the time we get to the corner my arm is down, and she's talking about her grandparents. "What if they too old or don't like me?"

She brings up a girl who came home with her and lived with Miss Saunders. Her grandparents said they wanted her. When she got there, they put her in foster care.

Char's eyes get big. "What if they send me home early?" she says, sounding nervous. "Or Miss Saunders's friend down there decide not to give me no job? It happened to Maleeka. People be changing their minds."

I pull her close, hold on tight. "Stop talking like that, girl." I mention her sister, JuJu, Maleeka, Mom. Tell Char they wouldn't let anything happen to her. "Me either." I can't hardly breathe with her arms around my neck. "Char. You choking me."

Char kisses me on the lips. Says, don't take it the wrong way. Her and me laugh, sit down on her steps one behind the other. She tricks me into saying I'll write to her at least four times this summer. I ask if she'll be my girlfriend coach.

"I'll leave that to Maleeka, 'cause you too messy." Then she apologizes for getting mad at me a little while ago. "I still got a temper . . . sometime anyhow."

Who don't know that?

Char stands up to go in the house. That's when we notice the little girl next door. On the porch. Combing her own hair. Crying. "I'll be back." Char unlocks her front door. Goes in, comes out carrying a case of brushes, combs, things in plastic bottles. "You want your hair braided, Jordyn?" Char says, on her way over there.

"Yeah."

Next thing I know, Char's talking to somebody through the screen door. "It's okay," she tells Jordyn. "Your mom said I could."

I watch Char part Jordyn's hair and scratch her scalp. Moisturize and comb her hair. Make straight, long rows to section it off. Brush and plait it. Beads and bows—red, yellow, blue—slide over her braids, end up in the middle on some of 'em and on the ends of other ones. Once she's done, Char holds up a mirror, lets her see herself.

"I got rainbows!" Jordyn shakes her head so the braids fly.

When Char's back, I tell her how good she is with kids. She brings up a little girl named Cricket that she took care of for a while. She got adopted a little while ago. Char writes her once a month, talks to her on the phone sometimes. "I used to think I wasn't good at nothing." She sits down behind me.

I'm good at everything. I keep that to myself.

She wants to own her own day care center, she tells me. "I already know what color the rooms gone be, the size of the groups, some of the learning toys I'ma buy."

Char's way different than she used to be. She could do anything she wants; I see that now. She made the dean's list three times this year. She was dumb as a doorknob in middle school. Maybe because her mother and father was killed, and her sister used to be wild.

Another man beeps at Char. Hanging out the window, he talk about her body like it's a car at the junkyard—only the parts matter to him.

I jump up. He laughs. Before I know it, I got my bow out. My arrow loaded, aimed at him.

"You ever shoot somebody with that?" Char asks.

I lie. "Almost."

"That's what I thought."

"But he don't know." I stare him down.

"You point it at the right person, and . . ."

"And what, Char?" I lower the arrow. "'Cause, like, I'm the only one looking out for you, far as I know."

"Did I ask you to?" She tells me to put my stuff away because she is tired of trouble.

It goes off without me meaning it to. Just missing his

windshield. Ending up on a porch across the street. After he drives off, I ask Char if she gets tired of creeps like him.

"You get used to it." She walks up the steps of her house.

"Girls shouldn't. Get used to it, I mean."

"Maleeka got used to me and you."

"Me? What I do?"

She does that rap song I made up about Maleeka in middle school. Then she frowns, when she laughed right along with the rest of us back then.

"Ah, that wasn't nothing, Char."

She talks about how we bullied Maleeka. But I wasn't no bully. Me singing that song wasn't nothing like what she did to Maleeka. I'd tell her that, but I need to get my arrow. Char's up the steps with the key in the lock when she says I should apologize.

"Me?" I point to myself. "To who? For what?"

"You clueless, John-John."

I tell her I don't owe anybody anything. That I'm tired of apologizing for stuff I ain't do in the first place. I cross the street and get my arrow off that porch. It's back in my case when I hear a woman's voice ask if I'm Big John's boy. She's sitting at the window, behind the screen. Old.

"Yeah." I squint to get a better look at her.

"Thought so."

Her name is Janie Lanie. Her family moved off our block soon after I was born, she tells me. Not that I'd remember. After she asks how Mom is and what Dad is up to, she gets back to me. There's enough shooting and killing around here, she says, without our boys coming up with new ways to hurt each other. I try to explain that it went off accidentally. That mostly I use it for fun. She asks if a person could put an eye out with that thing. "Yeah," I say. Then I correct myself. "Yes, ma'am."

"Then we don't need it in this neighborhood, nothing like it."

CHAPTER 35

MISS LANIE BEAT me home. She called Mom before I got there, told everything she seen and heard me say or do. Soon as I'm in the house, Mom gets Dad on the house phone in the kitchen. Putting Dad on speaker, she tells my father he needs to talk to me.

Sometimes they tag team me. Any day of the week, she'll put aside what she thinks he's done to her in order to save me from myself, Mom's good for saying. "I told your father what Miss Lanie said."

I turn my back on her. Pull open a drawer and take out the pie cutter. Slicing myself a piece, I talk about how Mom said I should look out for girls in our neighborhood.

"That's not what I told you!" She puts the phone to her ear. "I didn't say that, John. You know I wouldn't. JJ got a hard enough time taking up for himself. How's he gonna look out for somebody else?" Her hand covers the part you listen through, which don't make sense. "You wanna get yourself killed?" She asks where I got the archery set. Says it goes in the trash today. "No. Into the incinerator at work."

We argue for a while. Bending down, letting the dogs lick pie off my fingers, I ask Mom why she's making such a big deal out of this anyhow.

My father butts in. "That's the problem. The boy thinks he's the man of the house. And here you are trying to stick him on a bus full of books. Ain't that nice."

I look up at Mom. Right after Miss Lanie called, Mom tells me, she reached out to Miss Saunders and told her I was taking that job.

"Caleb said they hired somebody. They don't need me now."

Dad thinks I should come work for him. I'd end up with muscles, money in the bank, and so many girls I couldn't count 'em all, he says.

I'm wondering if he knew this would happen. Me doing something stupid. Mom calling him. So he could force me into working for him. "Naw." I wave my hands, shake my head no, like he can see. "I'm still looking for the right job."

What I say gets my mother madder than mad. "Move, y'all, please!" She looks at the dogs around her legs looking up at her. "Out my kitchen!" she hollers, like this is all their fault.

They run and hide. I pick up my pie and eat it in three bites. If I let him, Dad says, he'll make every boy in this hood wish they were his son.

"John, I didn't call you so you could fill his head with non-sense." Mom stops him this time when he interrupts. "Please. Just explain how dangerous it is for him to walk around with that thing."

I'd probably hurt myself before I hurt anyone else, I hear my father say. "But the police—" They're the ones I need to worry about, he thinks. That said, he wants it to stay in the house from here on out. It's a backyard thing anyhow, he tells us. Something for the park sometimes, but definitely not the streets. "Who don't know that?"

He gets back to me working for him. I'm almost out the room when Mom asks where I got it in the first place. Him and me got nothing to say. You don't snitch around here. I tell on him when I need to. Right now, I don't need to. I like archery. I feel strong when I shoot. Cool, carrying equipment. One day I'm gonna show Ashley what I can do with it.

In between the living room and dining room, I tell Mom that me and Caleb can practice using it in the park. She asks if I lost my hearing. "'Cause you must've if you ignoring what I just said."

I'm wondering how we got here. I was walking a girl home. Now Mom's talking about burning my stuff. "I paid for it." I don't know why I say it. "I'm keeping it." I sit on the floor. Two dogs jump in my lap. The other ones lie beside me. "Tell her, Dad."

My father wasn't a nice boy, he says. By eighteen, he was living on his own. Couch surfing. By his nineteenth birthday, he lived in California under a dock on the beach. I heard the story before. "And look how I turned out." The Chamber of Commerce is gonna give him an award soon after school starts because of how much business he does and how good he is at employing people from our neighborhood, he tells us. He takes boys and turns 'em into men, he says. "But your mother . . . she think she can do it better."

One.

Two.

Three.

That's how many seconds it takes before they're fighting. It's almost always about me. "He's taking that book truck job," Mom says." He'll start next week. They had problems getting a driver, so things got pushed back." Mom stands over me. "And the boy they gave the job to first, quit." Her eyes are on me when she says kids is just plain lazy these days.

"That truck goes to some rough neighborhoods, you know!" my father shouts.

Mom rolls her eyes and walks across the room. "You work in some rough neighborhoods."

But if something went down he'd be there for me, he tells her.

"I know how to fight," I say.

If she had let him keep me in those boxing classes, I would, Dad says. Boys who box get killed too, she tells him. Ones with knives and guns end up in the grave all the time, Mom reminds Dad. She keeps on talking. "I'm glad he uses his brains . . . enjoys reading . . . gets As in class."

My father is getting madder and madder. "Don't make him count how many of those boys end up in graves," he yells.

CHAPTER 36

MALEEKA WAS WITH Char when she told me something that made me feel like I was walking with no gravity involved. She gave Ashley my number. I couldn't sleep last night thinking about it. At like midnight, I asked Maleeka when she passed it on. "The last day of school," she told me.

School's been out two weeks.

I hate my life.

CHAPTER 37

WALKING LIKE HIS legs is made of iron, Caleb turns up the block. Even from here, I see dirt on his clothes, mud caked on his boots. His hair looks gray instead of light brown. His eyebrows too by the time he's standing in front of me. Halfway up his front porch steps he sits down. "You shoulda told me—" He leans his head against the railing. "Everything hurts."

"Told you not to work for my father."

Caleb and me ain't talked in a while. Not much anyhow. After that fight I just stayed away. Then Miss Lanie made things worse. So, I'm here.

"I almost quit today," he says, "but I really need the money." In a little while, he's snoring.

"Caleb." I shake the railing.

"What?"

"I need to talk to you." I tell him about Ashley.

"Find somebody else."

"But I like her, a lot."

"I like money, so?" He leans his elbows on his knees, opens and rubs his eyes. "I saw someone stealing from your father. Wrenches and other tools. But I didn't say anything because I'm new. Maybe next time—"

"Next time keep your mouth shut too. Make that money.

Get paid." My father got insurance. Plenty of it. And he's used to things walking off the job, I tell Caleb. "Besides, he'll find out who's doing it. He always does." I jump up. "Hey, is it because I'm short?"

Stretching, he stands up. "What?"

"I thought about it all last night. What if it ain't her mother? What if it's me? Too short."

Caleb goes down the steps real slow, like all his bones hurt. Stopping on the sidewalk, he bends down and touches his toes like he in gym class. His hands go up and up. Next thing I know, he's in front of the yard, by the fence like he's waiting on me.

"What if it's because I'm dark?" I say, when I get there.

"You've always been dark, right?"

"Don't be funny. You don't got my problems." I'm right behind him when he opens the gate. "Light-skinned people never do."

From the middle of the yard, he tells me there's plenty of girls out there that like short, dark dudes. He names three at school that got more girls than they can count. I forgot about them. He ain't forgot about how I teased Maleeka about being dark-skinned, he says. "If Ashley doesn't want you because of your color, it could be karma, right?"

I hope not. I don't like karma. She mean.

Opening the shed, he says it's probably just her mother. But that when a girl's got a mother like hers, you might as well quit while you're ahead. "Find yourself another girl, John-John. There's plenty in this neighborhood." He sound like Maleeka.

I remember the promise I made to myself at the beginning of the year. Get kissed. Get a girlfriend before school ends. None of it happened. Char doesn't count. And I remember what my mother said about that truck going everywhere, me meeting new people. "Am I too nice? That it?"

Caleb brings out the mower.

"You serious?" I ask.

"Are you helping me or not?"

That wasn't my plan. Him mowing means me bagging up the grass it leaves behind. It's the same at my house when it's my turn. "Your grass looks good to me."

Caleb pulls the string on the mower a few times. The engine starts, then stops. They need a new lawn mower. His father's been saying that for a while. I offer to go get ours if Caleb drives me.

He tries again. And again. And again.

"Move out the way." One try and I get it to start.

He goes up one row mowing, down the other. Then walks over to the fence and sits in the grass. You can tell he's thinking. Maybe it's about a new mower. Could be about his father—he ain't checked on him yet. "John-John."

"Yeah?"

"Could you finish for me?"

"Finish? I could do this lawn, the one next door, and the one up the street in ten minutes using one arm," I say. Then I get serious. "You know I got you, right?"

Caleb brings up our fight and apologizes.

"You ain't win," I say, lifting my fists. "You can't. Not against me." I dance on my feet, hit the air.

He's so tired, he don't answer. He sits against the fence with his head down. And just like that, he's snoring. At home, I don't mow as good as I could. But when Caleb helps me, our lawn looks like it got done by a professional. I take my time today. Every row is straight and even. All the clippings get put into green plastic bags. The bags get hauled over to the shed for trash day. He's still asleep by the fence when I open the gate and leave.

CHAPTER 38

THREE THINGS HAPPEN at the same time. The bookmobile beeps outside our house. Dad calls. Mom leaves the room. I got my phone in my hand, patting the dogs goodbye when Dad brings up some of the neighborhoods I might go to. He tells me to not let nobody take advantage of me.

"Dad . . ." I think about my equipment. Pretend it's strapped on my back. "I got this."

He brings up Mr. Junior's sons. They call themselves Twins Plus One. There's T-One, T-Two, and T-Three. They make good money throwing house parties on the weekends, he says. "Earning back-to-school money for college. Maybe you should start something like that."

"No. Mom wouldn't let me throw parties for money anyhow."

For once, he don't say nothing. Mom does though. "JJ. The truck's here." She's leaning out the front window.

Mom reminds me that she's having a meeting tonight at our house with other women from the block. It's about neighbors chipping in for a block party, cars parking on the sidewalk, the streetlight on our block still out, things like that. Dad always says he knows everything going on in our neighborhood. I think she knows more.

"Gotta go, Dad," I say, ready to end the call.

"You at the age where you should have all the fun you can, JJ. Old age is waiting right around the corner. Ask my knees."

I feel old sometimes myself. Caleb says he does for sure. Too much be happening in the world. It wears you down. Mom calls for me again. Dad's still pushing me to quit acting like a kid, telling me to not be old at the same time. How you do that?

Walking out the door, I think about Ashley, the boy from the library, and other boys who probably think she's pretty. Somebody's gonna see her, hold her hand, kiss her this summer maybe, and it won't be me.

You a McIntyre man, Dad always reminds me. "We always get what we want."

"Not me." It just comes out.

"'Bout time though, ain't it?" I can almost hear him say.

CHAPTER 39

DIDN'T MISS SAUNDERS say I would be working with a young person? Then why is some old man dressed like a pickle standing outside our house wearing green sneakers—cheap ones—light green pants—too short for him—and dark green round eyeglass frames? That ain't all. He got a snakeskin watchband on—green—and he's carrying a green coffee cup in his hand. My reputation is getting worse every day.

I go down the steps ready to shake hands anyhow. Looking like he's sucking a pickle, he says, "Punctuality is important in this job."

But he's late, not me.

"I'm Mr. Young. Not Mike. Not MB or 'hey, you.'" He shakes my hand.

"Good morning. I'm John." Mom told me not to use initials or nicknames at work.

He moves quick, fast in those green sneakers "Let's start by giving you a tour." Next thing I know we're at the back of the bookmobile, and he's unlocking it.

There's a rug on the floor, blue. And rows of books on both sides of the truck. The shelves are labeled. Fiction. Nonfiction. Science. History. Teens. Picture books. He asks if I know the difference between fiction and nonfiction.

"Yes, sir."

"You'd be surprised how many people don't."

He's a retired librarian. Miss Saunders told me that. Now his job is to drive the truck and help get books into people's hands, he says. My job is to assist him.

"I'll keep track of which people took which books," he says.

I laugh. "Don't nobody return library books, so why would they return these?"

"We know most books won't be returned. And that's good."

"That's not what librarians tell us at school."

"If somebody doesn't return a book, I'd like to think they enjoyed it so much they could not bear to part from it." For the first time he smiles. "Books can heal the world, you know. Literacy too."

The only man I know who talks like this is my English teacher, Mr. Jones. All last year, we laughed at him. The last day, I got what he was doing. Not imitating nobody else. Being hisself, no matter what. Dad wants me to be different from who I am. In the truck, my father texts me. Did he tell me that Mr. Junior and his wife are taking their sons and their girlfriends to Mexico for summer vacation? I can bring whoever I want when we go eat out sometimes, he says.

I put away my phone because Mr. Young tells me to. Just to make conversation, I ask if he lives near here. "Not too far away," he says on his way to the front of the bookmobile. His neighborhood might as well be in another country it's so different from around here. They got every kind of store you can name, Starbucks, sneaker stores. Two bakeries. A couple of restaurants. White people. And people like him I guess—men who dress like crocodiles and don't have a problem with it.

He gets in the truck, closes the door, and puts on his seat belt. I get in next. He straightens the rearview mirror. At the end of every day, we got to fill out a report for the organization, he tells me. "To let them know how many people we served and how many books were distributed to which area of the city. The information gets collected and passed on to the funders, plus area churches, libraries, and mosques."

"Why?"

"Statistics help us to prove that people in these communities want what other communities want—books for their children, for starters."

Driving off my block, he gives me the rules. "No talking or using phones for any reason, or bringing friends onto the vehicle." There's a camera onboard, watching everything we do. He points to it. "It doesn't miss anything. Neither do I." He tells me this will be an easy day for me. "Fun." But I know it won't.

CHAPTER 40

AT THE FIRST stop, there's a line of people waiting. Little girls. Old ladies. A man in a electric wheelchair and two girls around my age. I think about what Caleb said. What my father says sometimes. "Plenty girls be out there, son. Ain't no reason you shouldn't have two, three, shoot, ten even." Maybe if I could get one, he'd leave me alone.

They aren't as good-looking as Ashley. But if she was interested she woulda contacted me by now. Why girls play games?

All you need is one, I say to myself. *One girl to go out with you this summer. Not ten, you ain't that kind. That'll show Dad and Ashley too.*

"Is it possible for us to have just a bit more room, please?" Mr. Young says when people crowd around him at the back of the bookmobile. He makes them make room for him.

Jiggling the lock, he says something under his breath and finally gets it off. Once the door is open, he pushes a button to let down the wheelchair ramp.

I keep my eyes on them girls. Soon as they get to the front of the line, I wink. They smile. That was easy.

Things get crazy on the bookmobile. Everybody's talking. Reaching. Asking for what they want or for help with something. The man in the wheelchair rolled over my big toe. I kept my mouth shut and my eyes on them. The tall girl mostly. Her and her friend laugh a lot. Whisper a lot. End up standing next to me after a while. Except for Char and Maleeka, it's hard for me to think of things to say around girls, unless I'm being funny. I quit staring at the tall one and say what I'm thinking. "I like your shorts. They're so tight you probably need help getting 'em off."

She's smiling. She likes what I said, I can tell. Not Mr. Young. Right when I ask for her number, he excuses hisself and leaves the woman he was helping. Pulling me by my arm, he makes me get off the bookmobile. "On there"—he points at the truck—"we respect boundaries and other people's bodies. And you better not forget it."

I get an earful from him. And for what, saying I like some-body's clothes? Why girls wear 'em so short and tight if they don't want boys commenting? I'd ask, but Mr. Young ain't in the mood for no questions. The whole truck can tell that.

CHAPTER 41

DAY TWO ON the bookmobile sucks as bad as day one. Mr. Young's eyes followed me like I was a thief at Walmart. This time, I stay away from girls. I'm not good with them anyhow. It's like we speak different languages. My yes is their no. Their no is . . . I don't know what it is. But my eyes, that's different. How am I gonna control those? They got their own mind. Plus, I got to look at girls if I'm gonna say *good morning, can I help you*, or *yeah, I'll get that book off the top shelf for you*. Otherwise, I wouldn't be doing my job.

CHAPTER 42

FINALLY, A GOOD day at work. Maybe because Mr. Young was busy drinking coffee up front and doing some paperwork. Six elementary school boys are the last ones on the bookmobile. I explain the system to them. Explain my job when they ask. "Who made y'all come?" I say.

They all answer at the same time, "Nobody."

I think about Miss Saunders recruiting boys for our school. Ask 'em if they ever heard of it. If they knew where our school is located? In between, I can see Ashley's mom's face. She thinks she's right about boys from around here. She don't know nothing about us.

I get off the bookmobile with them after they get their books. "See, that's our school. The big building."

"The glass one?" a boy with freckles asks. I can tell he's gonna grow up to be short like me.

"My mother and father said I have to go there. I don't have a choice," the boy in blue shoes says.

I talk about some of the clubs. Our teams. The cafeteria and swimming pool. The end-of-the-year trips seniors go on. Last year they went to France. Next year it's Spain.

The boy named Maccoby never heard of Spain. I get back on the truck and find a book about countries around the world.

The other day, I told Mr. Young no one ever asks for it. That it's taking up space and we should get rid of it. Sitting on the sidewalk, I help them find France and Spain, Africa too because that's where human beings started from, I tell 'em. They never heard that last part. I let them know Africa isn't a country, like some people think. "It's a continent. There's seven of those." I name three. They name the rest. "Y'all smart. Better come to our school. A bunch of smart kids go there."

When the truck starts up again, Mr. Young says I should be a librarian or a teacher. "You were very good with those young men."

I don't exactly trust him, like I don't trust Ashley's mother. Tomorrow he might accuse me of something else.

CHAPTER 43

CALEB GOT PAID. We're at the pharmacy, in line, so he can put money down on the electric and gas bills. After he's done, I offer to treat him to lunch. He won't let me pay. Wish he did, the place we end up at used cheap meat in their burgers. Feels like little stones in my mouth when I chew. Soon as we finish eating, Caleb's got his calculator out, adding up numbers.

Everything is upside down from this side of the table, but I still can read it.

Gas: $1,650. Water: $636.25. Electricity: $2,225.90. Mortgage: $8,897.23. Maleeka: $20.

"What's that twenty dollars for by Maleeka's name?" I ask. "You owe her?"

"It's all I have," he says.

"For what?"

"To take Maleeka out."

"You about to not have a girlfriend."

Maleeka and her mother been in Florida all week. They went on vacation with Mr. Porter. Caleb says his mother told him there's plenty you can do on a date with twenty dollars. She's wrong, but I don't tell him. I ask when Maleeka's coming back.

"Monday, I think." He puts down his pencil.

"Have you ever been to Randy's Ice Cream Parlor?" Caleb asks.

I figure he wants to take her there. He could get two cones for two dollars each, no doubles though, I tell him. "And still have some money left over."

"Ashley's working there."

Her name is my favorite instrument, a drum, making my heart beat fast. For sure, I wouldn't tell anybody, but it does.

"I'll drive you when I get the time, if you wanna go." I'd be so nervous I might crash, he tells me.

"For real?"

"I owe you for mowing my lawn and helping me with my father. So I talked to Maleeka. She talked to Char. They got her number, I don't know how."

"I owe all y'all now."

He stands up and starts saying numbers. It takes me a minute to realize it's a phone number.

"Hers?"

Caleb don't answer. I'm dancing like I got a partner. Like I'll never stop. People are looking at me, but I don't care.

"You doing all this over a phone number?" my father would say.

Yep.

CHAPTER 44

I AIN'T DESPERATE. I don't think so anyhow. But soon as I get home, I call her. "Hey, Ashley."

"John. You still sound the same."

"Do I?"

It's a long time before she says, "Yes."

I lie on the bed. "Is that good or bad?" Put my feet on the wall.

She laughs. "Good. Real good."

I get down on the floor 'cause I can't keep still. My feet end up on my headboard and I put a pillow underneath my head. "Good." I close my eyes. *'Cause I like you. You like me?* I let the question stay in my head because I'm scared what her answer might be.

I hear a bus driver tell people to step back so he can let more people on. I think she's one of those people.

"John?"

"Yeah."

"I have to go."

"Yeah. I know."

I ask what she does on the way to work. It's a stupid question. "Read." Ashley says she's read two books since school let out. "What about you?"

"Me?" I sit up and explain that when it comes to reading, I mostly read instruction manuals after Mom buys something that I need to put together. "And books for class. But I don't read all that much for fun."

"But you're in the library a lot."

"Listening to books, remember. Not stories and stuff. But like . . ." I don't tell her. I can't. It would sound dumb. I like books about trees, archery, how fast a baseball goes in the rain or the dark. Once I listened to a book about bees. It was interesting.

"Well . . . listening to a book is reading. I think."

Mom says it's not.

After she's gone, I go to the bathroom, run warm water in the tub and add bubbles. Not that I would tell anybody.

CHAPTER 45

ANOTHER BAD DAY at work, and it wasn't my fault, no matter what Mr. Young thinks. So, I'm here at Miss Saunders's office, trying to handle my business. To try and see in her face if she's on my side or not. I begin with today, Friday, and work backward to the day I first started a couple of weeks ago. "And then"—I stop to catch my breath—"he said strike one." I'm up again. "What's that mean, Miss Saunders? Do those girls get strikes?"

"For doing what, John?"

"I don't know. But they did something. I got blamed for it."

"All of them?"

"Well—"

Pretty ain't no crime, Maleeka said to me one time. And just because a girl is pretty, it don't mean boys get the right to say what they want, do whatever they please. Both her and Char told me that a couple days ago. "I made a joke. They laughed. They liked it, Miss Saunders."

"I understand, John."

I lean my elbows on my lap and move in closer. "You do?"

She asks how the rest of my time there has been going.

"Didn't he tell you?"

"No. Maybe he wanted to handle things."

Today, those little boys came back. One of 'em said he liked this girl but he was too afraid to get her number. I asked her because I see her all the time. And she's little, like a sixth grader—why would I want her number?

Miss Saunders asks me to slow down, breathe. She gets up and comes back with soda and snacks. I can't even eat or drink, I'm so upset.

"You're at work, John, when you're on the bookmobile. Being paid. Try to remember that."

I open my mouth to defend myself. But she outtalks me. "Did Mr. Young tell you he has six daughters?"

"Six?"

"Yes."

He only talks about work. About me and what I do wrong, I tell her. "I'm thinking about quitting."

Maybe sometimes Mr. Young overreacts, she tells me. But that doesn't mean I haven't crossed some lines or hadn't done so another time, she thinks. With her eyes on mine, she stands up. "Is it possible?"

I stand up too. "Is what possible?"

"That you crossed a line. Or got extremely close to it."

I'm ready to say no. To spell it out for her. To scream it. When she puts her fingers up to her lips. "Think about each incident."

"Incident?"

She says for me to close my eyes and try to recall them in as much detail as I can.

I don't get no pictures. But I hear my words. "Well . . ." I listen to 'em again. "I guess . . ." I try to see their faces. "Every single one of them girls was smiling, Miss Saunders, I swear they were." Then I remember the little girl. She kept moving away. It didn't mean much to me because, well, she a kid. I could be her older brother. "Girls give you mixed signals." I sit down.

Regardless, she tells me, I need my own line. A way of behaving that don't change from girl to girl, minute to minute. "We all need those. That way everyone is sure of what they can expect of other people and of themselves too." It's called boundaries, she says.

I think about Ashley, Char, and Maleeka. I'm always respectful with them. Middle school was different though. I played around a lot. Maybe I went too far in a different way making up songs about Maleeka, saying whatever I wanted to her.

CHAPTER 46

HE HITS THE target. Makes a bullseye. Not that we celebrate or nothing. It's one of those days. I can see on his face it's got something to do with his dad. I would normally ask about Mr. P. But I just can't today.

Snatching the arrow out the target, Caleb hands it over to me. Yells when he talks, practically. "Look at the tip," he says, rubbing it. "Dull. If I had the money"—he hands it over—"I'd have my own set."

I ask what happened. Turns out it wasn't his father. It's got something to do with money. He paid on that electric bill but a lot less than he shoulda, not on purpose though. Now they have to pay a penalty and his mom had to make new arrangements with the company. "I don't usually make mistakes, especially when I'm handling things for my parents."

He mentions something Maleeka said to him. About his clothes. He ain't been ironing them because they're work clothes, dirty by the end of every day, he tells me. The ones he's got on could use a washing, not that I say so. "Dad changes out of his clothes before he gets home. Showers at his office. He'd let you do that."

After work, he goes home, helps out. Cooks sometimes, especially if his mom is working a triple shift. Plus, he's working for my father and mowing lawns to earn extra money, whenever he gets a chance. "Could she do the bills?" I ask.

She talks to the companies. The doctors. The hospital. Figures out what they can and can't pay, he tells me. "On top of taking care of Dad and working all the time." He picks the skin off his nails. "I'm doing what my father would do until he can do it himself." Then he says that the one thing he wants more than anything now is to be rich. Who don't want that?

CHAPTER 47

I THINK MILDRED is dying. She's our oldest, been with us the longest. When I get home, she's lying in the middle of the floor quiet and panting, not jumping up to meet me like usual. I don't think much about it until I notice the other dogs whimpering like they at a funeral.

"Mildred?" I get down on my knees. "You okay, girl?" I know she ain't. I can see it in her eyes. By the way she can hardly lift her paw. "Mom! Mom!" I get up and go to the bottom of the steps. "Mom! Where you at, Mom?!" She don't answer. I think about the basement, her washing clothes, and run down there. "Mildred's dying." I run back upstairs, sit on the living room floor beside Mildred. "It's okay, girl. I'm here." Her eyes open and close. I whisper in her ear. "If you need to go, I understand. But we don't want you to go, okay?"

A little while later, Mom comes in the house. It's like she don't even notice Mildred's head on my lap. "I was across the street. Another community meeting. Some kids been having parties and car mirrors got broken." When she brings up the broken streetlight, I stop her.

"She's dying."

Mildred. On her knees, she examines her. Takes her pulse. "I'm sorry, baby." She rubs my chin. "She's old and the cancer finally caught up to her, I guess." She rubs Mildred's fur. It used to be darker and thicker, Mom told me, when she first came to live with us. Now it's gray and black, falls out when it gets brushed. "Looks like we're gonna have another angel." Mom always says animals are angels that God puts on earth to help us love each other more, treat each other better. When they go people get their own personal angels. She really believes it.

Mildred's eyes stay closed while we pat and talk to her.

"Mom?"

"Yes."

I've been wanting to talk to her about everything that happened on that truck since I started. But my father is right about one thing. You can't tell her everything. I'm the man of the house. Gotta be strong for her. I go put on some jazz. Mildred likes it. I find her favorite blanket on my way back and cover her up. Then collect her favorite toys from all over the house. An hour later, Mom says it's time. We'll call a car to take us to the vet. She pinches my cheek. "You okay?"

I put my arm over her shoulder. "I got you, Mom."

"I know, JJ. I know."

In the car, on the way to the vet, Mom cries so hard, I'm surprised we both don't drown.

CHAPTER 48

I CALLED TO tell her about Mildred. Ashley got off the phone because her mother was coming. Late at night, while I was in my bed missing Mildred, Ashley wrote me.

Somebody might say she's only a dog. But she was part of your family. I know people say that boys shouldn't cry, but it's okay if you do, I think.

I didn't cry. I wanted to, but I didn't. I thought about Ashley the rest of the night. She woulda liked Mildred. Caleb did. In the park the next day, him and me talk about Mildred, and why he's so happy today. Caleb picked me up, smiling; talking more than me. He looked like his old self, with his pants clean, smelling like he showered. He hit the target twice in a row, scored well. Had some good news too. He hired somebody.

"Huh? What you talking about?"

He hits the target again. Caleb says he's been thinking about it since school let out. He could make more money if he could work more hours, but he can't work longer because he's just one person. "I hired Jaxxon."

He's in one of our classes, responsible.

Caleb's got it all figured out, how much he can pay himself and pay Jaxxon. How much he can save, and how many lawns

Jaxxon can mow in one weekend. Jaxxon said he could work eight hours on Saturdays and eight hours on Sundays for Caleb. "What else am I doing?" he told him. "Just working at McDonald's three days a week."

Caleb thinks he'll make a lot of money. "Then in the fall, I'll hire two more people."

"You still quitting school?"

"Yeah. Until my father is well, it's all about the money."

CHAPTER 49

IT'S EARLY. TOO early for Caleb to be calling me, waking me up. I pull the covers over my head. Silence my phone. Not that it stops him. It's vibrating, making me answer it anyway. "You up?" Caleb asks.

Why people ask you that when you're talking to 'em, which means you awake, don't it? "Yeah, I'm up."

His dad is in the hospital. Caleb's at the hospital too. Him and his mother are waiting for a neurologist to come on duty. He's supposed to be there around twelve. "I asked your father for extra hours. He said I could work three Saturdays this month, starting today." Caleb is worried my father will fire him for missing work.

Dad can be a jerk, but he isn't *that* bad, I say. "I seen him give plenty of guys extra chances."

He's been trying to reach my father. But Dad ain't answering. I don't even try on Saturday mornings, I tell Caleb. Not before eleven anyhow. It would have to be an emergency if I did. "That's our family time," I heard Sheila say once.

Ain't I family?

I never told Mom. She'd go off. I wanted to myself after I heard it. But my father made his choice. Picked a side. I got Mom anyhow.

I throw back the covers. "I know where Dad is." I change out of my underwear. Get into my bedroom slippers. "You want me to tell him about Mr. P.?"

"Explain that I had to come to the hospital. My mother gets too nervous to drive if she's alone with him. But it won't happen again. Tell him, okay?"

"Okay."

Before I know it, I'm in the shower washing my hair, behind my ears, and a few other places. I brush my teeth, then open my mouth under the sprinkler to rinse. Downstairs, I fry four eggs and make grits before I leave. I went to sleep hungry. Mom and the neighbors had another meeting. The dogs don't move a muscle when I leave.

CHAPTER 50

THE HOUSE MY father's working on ain't that far from ours. The people moved out and left everything—including two cats and a motorcycle in the basement, Dad told me. Stuff like that ends up in one of his garages. He found a home for the cats. His job is to empty everything out, strip the walls down to the studs. Another crew's gonna take over after that.

I get there right when my father's truck shows up. His workers climb out the back while I tell him about Caleb. Dad asks how Mr. P. is doing. I don't really know. I didn't ask. You in the hospital, you in trouble, that's what I think.

My father sticks a pair of tan work gloves in his back pocket. "You coming?"

I point to myself.

"Yeah, you?"

I'm going home to finish sleeping, I say, walking past him and a couple of his men. He follows me. "I thought you came to work off Caleb's time. To do right by your friend. Don't he need the money?"

"Yeah, he needs the money. But he's at the hospital. He'll be back Monday."

"And lose a whole day's pay?"

That's what happens if you don't show up for work, I almost say. "I gotta go, Dad."

"I'm trying to do right by that boy, JJ. What you trying to do?"

Me and Caleb wasn't all that close in middle school. But once we got to high school, things changed. Nerds wasn't all that welcomed at our old high school. You got bullied, tripped, threatened—called out your name on the bus—jumped. Dyeing my hair blond, getting a tat didn't make them accept me either. For the first time, I knew how Maleeka felt. I ate lunch in the library. Caleb came every day the same period. That told me everything. He ain't have to explain nothing. I started going to his house a lot after that. His mother cooks good. Mr. P. is easy to talk to, that's what I found out. And Caleb is a lot like me—he ain't no fighter. He just a nerd boy from the hood. And he's *the only one* I would do this for. "Just for today, Dad."

My father tells everyone to listen up. "This is my boy. He gets no special favors."

He walks up the steps and unlocks the door. I follow him in the house. They follow us. Dapping me up, they say hi. One man said he figured I was Dad's son. "Y'all the shortest bros in the city." The darkest too, I hear somebody say. He ain't have to go there.

Dad kept me away from work like this. I always got good grades. He didn't. Plus, this is a dirty job, he'd say, hard on your hands, your back, your joints. Old men in this business got twisted fingers, swollen knuckles. Dad ain't no exception. He wants me to be an engineer. To take over his business. I don't got the nerve to tell him I'm thinking of becoming a social worker. A lot of kids got problems—family beef and other bad stuff happening in their lives. They need somebody like me in school so they can still learn. People like Ashley's mom wouldn't understand.

"JJ."

"Yeah, Dad?"

"Stay close."

He moves fast. Talks fast. Points high, then low. Leaving men who supposed to be following him, my father goes from one room to the next. What's left of the furniture, he wants out now. The rugs and linoleum he wants pulled off the floor, cut up. I can't hardly keep up. He wants to know why I'm following him. "I gave my orders. Get busy."

Caleb owes me.

Dad reaches in his other pocket. "Here." It's a knife. One blade. Made for cutting carpet and rugs, people too, I guess.

It's in my back pocket when I start upstairs behind two men. Halfway up, I stop. Check for my wallet. It mighta dropped out my pocket. Up the street I pulled it out to check my money. It's old-school, but Mom believes you should keep some cash on you.

I jump over the banister. End up on a chair that falls over with me in it. Dad thinks I'm playing around. So I got to hear his big mouth. Listen to him yell at me in front all these men.

"We got protocols here, JJ! Safety rules!" He pulls a folded-up sheet of paper out his back pocket. "Read 'em. 'Cause these men wanna get home to their families just like me and you wanna get home to ours."

"I'm doing you and Caleb a favor, alright?" I go outside to find my wallet. Come back empty-handed. Somebody probably already got it.

What Dad told me to do when I first got here ain't what he wants done now. Get rid of the chair I ruined, he says. Guess I'm being punished. Most of the stuffing from the cushion was already gone. But the wooden arms and legs were in good condition, intact, he yells. I busted one of 'em. It was a antique, before I got to it, my father tells me. "I had a buyer. Now it's trash."

I wrap my arms around it. Before I get to the front door, I'm out of breath, my legs burn. That's why I stop and rest.

They watch everything I do. Dad too. This time when I lift the chair, I'm practically dying. They laugh when my father says some things you got to learn the hard way. Maybe this is what he means. The door is too narrow for the chair. I twist and turn it. Sit it down so it don't break my back. Climb over it. Go out the door to try to force it through. Then come back inside. A man wearing a I LOVE BEING ITALIAN T-shirt walks up to me. "I got you, little dude." He lifts it. Walks over to a window, throws it in the dumpster.

My father reaches for another chair, but I stop him. "I got this." Soon as I lift it, I feel my leg muscles get weak, my back muscles ache.

Resting, I watch cut-up pieces of rugs fly out the second-floor window into the dumpster. Broken stools, rusted pipes, and a desk go out the window next.

Standing beside me, my dad don't say a word. But he bends down when I bend down. Together we walk the chair across the living room, into the dining room, and throw it out the window. The dumpster is mostly empty, so when it hits, the noise hurts my ears. Accidentally, I slap my father five.

CHAPTER 51

EVERYTHING HURTS, EVEN my teeth. So, ain't no way I could make it to my room. I almost didn't make it into the house. I had to sit outside on the steps for a while. It coulda been ten or twenty minutes, I ain't sure. Dad told me the longer I stayed there the harder it would be to get up.

Mom brings a blanket to the couch, lays it over me asking if I'm hungry. I can't eat nothing. I got no strength. Dad's by the front door. "Legs feel like spaghetti, huh?" He laughs. Next thing I know, he's standing over me. "It'll get easier."

"For Caleb, maybe," Mom says on her way out.

My father pulls back the covers and gets down on his knees. Next thing I know, he's untying my sneakers. I should try to make it upstairs, he tells me. To get myself in the shower or soak for a while in the tub. "Epsom salts usually does the trick." He takes off one shoe, then the other. For a minute, he rubs my feet, my toes, and in between.

I close my eyes. They stay that way even after Mom brings me dinner and Tylenol. I can feel the tray on my thighs. They hurt too. My eyes stay shut when I ask her to take it away. They both laugh this time.

Mom offers me a bite of hot dog. I can't, I tell her. She

holds a carton of chocolate milk up to my mouth. I drink out the straw, fall asleep with milk in my mouth. When I wake up, my shoes are by the door. My socks are turned inside out, stuffed inside my boots like Dad does his after work every night, even while he lived here.

CHAPTER 52

DAD WAS RIGHT about Epsom salts. But I still come downstairs plenty sore. Mom's singing in the kitchen when I get there. Bacon's frying on the stove. I steal a piece off a plate on the table. And get two more pieces for the dogs. Today her and a coworker are going to the movies, Mom says, taking plates out the cabinet over the stove. I ask if it's a date.

"It's one of the younger college girls," she tells me. Mom found out she was thinking of taking a class at community college. So, she went with her to hear a presentation. "Just to check into things," she says, looking embarrassed.

At the table, Mom wipes syrup off the edge of my plate, then licks her finger. "Am I too old to go to college, JJ?"

"You not old, Mom."

I should tell her if I think she is, she says. "I was in the admissions office and everybody was so young."

"Miss Lanie is old, Mom. Not you."

She thinks she wants to be a veterinarian's assistant. Classes take two years if you go full-time; three to four if you go part-time, she says. "You'll be in college soon, JJ. We can't afford college expenses for us both."

Mom don't look sad much. Right now she does. I sit a plate on the floor for the dogs. They come running, pushing each other out the way, barking, swallowing oatmeal while it's still pretty hot.

I tell Mom how good she is with animals. How much they love her back. For some reason, Caleb pops in my head. I think about how much more money he'll make than me, especially with his business. "Mom. You think I shoulda took a job working with Dad?"

Her face twists up. "Working with who?"

"Come on, Mom."

She tells me to stop talking nonsense. That she just wouldn't feel right knowing I was at work tearing up houses, breathing in asbestos. "It just isn't safe. Do you hear me, JJ?"

"He said he needs somebody to replace Mr. Bill at the garage. I could work there."

"No, just no."

I start thinking about Ashley. Before the summer's over, we'll be dating, I know it. I wanna pay when she's with me. Some dudes wouldn't. But I ain't them. You need money when you got a girlfriend.

Mom brings up college again. She felt good being on campus, she says. "I went one semester a long time ago and dropped out."

If she goes this time, she'll finish, I know it.

Mom pinches my cheek, like always. "Enough about me. What about you?"

"What about me?"

"How's that girl?"

I almost lie. But this is Mom; I ain't got to. "I sent her a card, Mom." I don't say I sent it to her job after we talked about Mildred. "I got one back from her yesterday." I can't help smiling. Mom either.

"See. She likes you." She pinches me again. "Give her time."

I don't tell Mom how many times I read that thing. How at night, I pull it out and read it over and over with the moon shining on me like it do in the movies. I didn't say anything to Caleb or nobody else about it because with a mother like hers, Ashley might disappear on me. But a card or a letter, words on your phone are there forever, even when the person who sent 'em is gone for good.

"What about work?" Mom puts more food on my plate. "Mr. Young treating you okay?"

After Miss Saunders's talk, I went to him. "Could I get your rules in writing?" I said. By the end of the day, I had 'em. Next, I asked about his daughters. He said their names and gave me their ages. He told me that he retired early so he could be with them when they came home from school. They're grown now.

"It's a crazy world. You can't be too careful," Mr. Young said.

For the first time, I thought about Dad's daughter. Any boy thinking about dating her is gonna be in trouble.

CHAPTER 53

BEEN A WEEK and a half since I saw my dad, not that I missed him exactly 'cause sometimes he doesn't think about what he says to me. In the restaurant the last time, all he did was talk about the bumps on my face.

He changed up things for today anyhow. Home Depot's out. So is the restaurant. It's early. Her son is with him. Dad said he had to make a few runs and he wanted me to babysit. When I get in my father's car, I say, "You bring the cologne?"

"Yeah." He points to the glove compartment. "Every girl in this city is gonna want you after you spray this on."

It slips out. "I only need one, Dad."

That's my problem, he says. "You aim too low."

"Maybe you're just old." I look at Giovanni in the back seat, playing with toy dinosaurs.

Me and my father's wife got rules. I don't come to their house. That's her rule. She never said it to me out loud, I just know. I don't babysit or get nowhere near her kid. That's my rule. Only, I don't say it in front of him. Ever. He can't see clear when it comes to her. And I don't have time to make him. But I could use the money.

"Daddy—"

I used to call him that.

"Daddy. You drive too fast."

My father slows down and tells me that when he gets out the truck I'm to keep the engine running, the windows locked. "I paid my guys yesterday. There's a lot more money in the trunk."

Dad pays in cash. Most guys like it that way. I know Caleb does. Yesterday, Caleb took a picture of tens and twenties spread out on his bed. The medical bills, credit cards all paid on, but not caught up, he told me. "I dream about making money now."

My father parks near a three-story house with the bricks painted white. It's only ten o'clock in the morning and people sit on steps and the railing, playing cards, smoking cigars, holding beers. They talk and laugh loud. I keep my eyes on the people on the porch because I don't know them and they don't know me.

"Big John!" A man pushes the screen door open. "My man."

"Got something for me?" I hear my father say. He owns two garages full of equipment—riding mowers, backhoes, even a rowboat—just about anything you might need to fix a house inside or out or rent something because you don't own one. The garage next to that is full of old, dirty sinks, planks, windows, refrigerators, front and back doors in any color or size you want, boxes and boxes of bolts and nuts, springs and ceiling lights, railings, even a few refrigerators. Some of it he got on sale at Home Depot. Lots of it comes from houses he guts. People around here like to do business with him because they can pay by the week or a little at a time.

Giovanni unbuckles his belt and climbs into Dad's seat. "Play with me."

"No, I'm busy." I look at my phone.

He holds up two dinosaurs and growls. "This one is yours." He drops it in my lap.

I pick it up, sit it in the chair by his knee. Next thing I know, Giovanni climbs into my lap. "Little dude. Get in your own seat."

He puts his arms around my neck and leans all the way back until his head is on the dashboard. "I don't want a sister. I need a brother."

I keep quiet, until he starts crying. I pat his back. "Look, I'm playing, see." I pick up a dinosaur.

He asks where my sister is. I don't have one, I say. He asks where my brother is. It's mean, but I don't answer.

He points to himself. "I'm your brother, right? Mom says so."

"Right."

"You don't act like a brother," Char said once.

Because I'm not a real one. He don't come around me and I don't go around him, I told her.

"But he's a little kid, John-John," she said. "Grow up."

Giovanni puts out his right hand. "I told Justin that I have a brother just like him. He didn't believe me." Giovanni pats my face hard, with both his hands. "Can you tell him for me?"

"Tell him what?"

"That you're my brother. And I got one just like him." When it looks like he's gonna cry, I say, "Okay, I'll tell Justin." I figure he'll forget in a little while.

You'd think I gave him a birthday present, he hugs me so

hard and long. When he asks me to tell him a story, I almost say no. Until I think about what Char said.

Giovanni lays his head on my chest. His thumb goes into his mouth. His feet go on the dashboard. Lifting his other hand, he rubs my chin. I make up a story about a boy with six brothers who took him on a ride to the moon. I would tell myself that story when I was little all by myself in my room.

CHAPTER 54

IT'S JULY, ONE of those days, warm not hot, sky clear blue, like only good things can happen. So, Caleb and me ought not be surprised when a bunch of good stuff does happen to us, finally. Mr. P. got a good report from the doctor. They took him off one of his medicines. And Ashley called me. It was late when she did. After one. She woke me up. I sounded real sleepy, I guess, so she asked if she should call some other time.

"NO!" I apologized for hollering in her ear. "You can call me anytime. Day or night. Even in school," I said, lowering my voice so I didn't wake up Mom.

Two hours later I texted my father. *I know what you think about me, but you wrong. Girls do like me.*

He never sleeps so he got back to me fast.

I never said they didn't. Just that you needed to step up your cool. You think I'll be here forever. But I'm old. I need to know you gonna be alright once I'm gone.

Stop talking like that.

You'll see when you're old.

You be dressing young. Trying to act like you young.

Grow up, JJ. Dressing young ain't being young. I miss those days.

I miss how our family used to be, but I keep my mouth

shut. Not him. He still talking. Only he quits texting and dials my number.

"A man is supposed to be a provider," he says. "To make sure his family is safe and got what they need. I do that, nobody's ever had to tell me to."

"I know, Dad."

"I need to go, JJ." He sure sounds tired.

"Okay, Dad."

"We always end up fighting."

"You blaming me?"

"See what I mean."

"I just asked a question, Dad."

"A man can't say all he's thinking and feeling, you know."

I know. How come he thinks I don't know?

"Sheila say I don't do this with her or that with her boy . . . and the business . . . Never mind. What you know about taxes anyhow?" Under his breath he says, "A man can only do the best he knows how."

I hear him curse. It's about his knee. He's walking through the house, he says, and hit it on something. Like a minute later, Dad sounds different, like he's over there smiling. "You good, boy?" he says.

"Yeah. I'm good."

"Same here. Never been better."

CHAPTER 55

CHAR SHOULD BE gone by now. But her grandmother was in the hospital. Her trip almost got canceled. She's finally leaving for Alabama tomorrow. I'm sitting between her legs, waiting for her to braid my hair, watching the girl next door reading a book from our bookmobile. How come y'all don't come on our block? Char asked the other week. "Kids here read too."

We can't be everywhere, I told her. The next day she showed up with four kids, plus Jordyn from next door. Char told me I looked like a professional in my khakis and white button-up shirt. She asks if I still hate working on that truck.

"I'm still there, ain't I?"

Char pulls and pinches hair near my neck. "Ouch, Char. Not so hard."

"You know I'm about to leave."

I came to say goodbye, and for her to braid my hair. I offered to pay, thinking she wouldn't take it. I was wrong.

Char will leave tomorrow on the six o'clock plane. Maleeka and her said bye yesterday, because Maleeka's mother found a gown in Virginia and she thinks she might want to buy it. They left this morning, with her almost-stepfather driving.

"I'll miss you, Char."

She gives me a warm kiss on the back of my neck.

"I knew you liked me."

A hard comb knocks me upside the head.

"I still think you like me, Char."

Getting back to her trip, she says she's looking forward to spending time with family and working. Before she stands up, she says for me to be good. "Because bad things can happen even if you ain't looking for it."

"I know." I stare up at her. "Char."

"Yeah."

"What you think about me? The way I look, I mean?"

I'm short, she says, laughing right along with me. "Handsome." Her voice is sweet and soft as dough when she says for me not to let nobody make me feel like I ain't good enough. "You hear me, John-John?"

"I hear you."

"Boys be so hardcore and tough, people act like y'all don't got no feelings. That y'all don't want some of what us girls want . . . somebody to like you, to be nice to you no matter what you look like, how much you weigh, or where you come from." She sits beside me, close enough for her soft, sweet-smelling skin to rub up against mine.

She wasn't always nice, she tells me, like I don't know. But she ain't deserve the things that happened to her, she says. And we didn't have the right to treat Maleeka the way we did. "You gone find the right girl, John-John. And you gonna know she the right one 'cause she's gonna treat you good. Not like how we treated Maleeka. But if Ashley or any other girl act like she don't wanna be bothered. Or says no I don't like you or wanna date you. Believe her, John-John. Leave her alone.

Find somebody else to treat you the way you want to be treated."

Char's got a pretty smile. How come I'm just finding that out? And she's smart about a lot of things. I mention it to her. Girls mature faster than boys, she tells me. "Plus, I'm older than you." I act way younger than her, Caleb, and Maleeka, she says. "But I guess that's not such a bad thing . . . being a kid long as you can, I mean."

CHAPTER 56

CALEB'S ALL ABOUT that money. He helped his mother pay off her Macy's bill last week. Put down six hundred on the house, which equals twelve hundred with the money his mother added to it, he said the other day. Caleb said he'd take me to see Ashley this week. He told me to meet him at his house so we could talk about it. Then he changed his mind. Now I'm meeting him at a house two blocks from ours where he'll be working. I get there and, man, that lawn is two lawns in one, it's so big. He's already almost done. Hope they paying him good.

He's not wearing a shirt. His back is sweaty, red like it's on fire. Pushing that mower uphill, you see how much bigger his muscles got. Maybe I need to mow more.

Caleb stops to move a rock out the way. The next time he stops, it's to empty the bag that holds the grass. It's a new mower. He got it from Dad. Paid for it in cash. Not a lot. Dad bought it used. He oiled and cleaned it up for Caleb, Caleb tells me once he's done.

"Your father has two more mowers I want to buy. Maybe in a couple of years, I can buy property around here too."

"You mean a house?"

He's been talking to my father, he says. "He knows a lot."

"He talks a lot."

"I could be a millionaire by twenty-two." Walking his mower over to his car, Caleb only talks about money. He points to a house across the street. "How much do you think it costs?"

"I don't know."

"I do."

I go to get in the car, and he stops me. "Let me wash up and meet you at your house."

"You shoulda said that before I walked here."

"I got a lot on my mind."

CHAPTER 57

WALKING HOME, I run into my father. I didn't see him at first. He pulled onto somebody's sidewalk right behind me like he was the police. His window was down by the time I got to the car. "Need a ride?"

I'm sweating as much as Caleb was. "Sure."

He got the air conditioner on high. A bottle of cold water in the cup in between us, like he was expecting me. He takes off the top. "Here." Dad pulls into traffic and speeds up.

I got a mouthful of cool water when he invites me to a picnic at his house two weeks from now.

He's cooking, he says, opening and closing his right hand like it hurts. "You can bring that girl if you want."

"Next time."

"Or Char or Maleeka—I don't care."

I think about our last conversation. Maybe I can do better, who knows. He did just say I could bring Ashley. That's something.

We around the corner from my house when Dad says, "Oh, I been meaning to let you know that whatever you said to Giovanni . . . thanks."

"I didn't say nothing."

"Since Saturday he keeps talking about his big brother."

Dad puts his hand on my shoulder. "Now he can't wait to be a big brother."

I wanted to be a big brother when I was little. It never happened. Dad asks what I think about him.

"Giovanni? He likes dinosaurs. That's all I know."

"He's got sixty if he's got one, I swear." Dad raises his hand like he's in court.

I take a long drink. And ask him if he remembers when I had a bunch of little cars all over the house. "I had more than sixty. Maybe a hundred, what do you think?"

"At least. The dog swallowed one, remember? The vet bill cost us about three hundred dollars."

Him and me are in front of my house parked, laughing. He brings up Mom. I never knew she didn't want me to have those cars. "You were five. The package said you should be seven or eight to have them." Every time Mom came home I had another one, he says. "Sometimes a man knows better what a boy needs."

Dad asks if I still have them. I never throw things away. "Somewhere," I say, turning on the radio. Finishing my water.

"Have you seen Caleb lately?"

"A little while ago, why?"

"He didn't tell you?"

"You tell me. You brought it up." I put the top on the empty bottle.

"The city put an eviction notice on their front door."

You got to be way behind in your mortgage to get one of those, even I know that.

"Maybe Caleb doesn't want you to know."

"But we're friends."

Even friends got secrets, he tells me. Same as married couples. "Let him bring it up when he's ready."

Dad was right about secrets. Caleb ain't tell me something else too. Him and Maleeka broke up. Maleeka lets me know after I call her about the house. Only I don't get to tell her about it at first. "I love Caleb. But I remember how it was when my father died," she said. "All I could think about was my mother and making sure she was alright. I didn't care about anybody else." He doesn't either, she told me. "I ain't mad at him. I just can't be with him."

After she said it, I brought up the house. She hadn't heard either. But Maleeka wasn't surprised that Caleb kept it to himself, she said. "Lately Caleb tells you only what he wants you to know. And he doesn't want you to know much about what he's up to, I think."

CHAPTER 58

I NEVER KNEW a family that was put out of their house before. Thinking about it, I couldn't sleep. Mom asked why I kept getting out the bed and going downstairs. I told her I was thirsty, not that I'm worried about Caleb. It was like two in the morning when I went out back and sat on the porch in the dark, wondering if Caleb's gonna be homeless.

First thing I do on Sunday is go to his house. The door's open, wide. Maybe they did it to hide the notice. Guess it could be to let in some air. Air conditioners cost a lot of money to run. Mom says that a lot.

I walk in. Caleb's on the couch, stretched out with a book on his stomach. His father is in the wheelchair with a book too. "Hey, Caleb, you wanna go to the park?" I sit on the arm of the couch.

"Nope."

"New couch?" I wish I hadn't said that as soon as it's out my mouth. It don't look new, it looks used, older than the one that was here since I been coming.

They started a book club, his father tells me, looking embarrassed. "It was Caleb's idea."

"That ain't fun, Mr. P. That's like schoolwork. Tell Caleb what you said about fun."

Moving slow, he reaches for Caleb's hand, patting it like he's a little boy. "Go, Caleb. It'll . . . it'll make me happy."

I look at Mr. P. real good. "You okay? You look funny."

He sticks his left hand under his blanket. Says the bruises came from a IV when he was in the hospital yesterday. The cuts on his neck and chin came from shaving.

"I told my father I can do that." Caleb sits up.

"I need . . . to do . . . some things . . . for myself."

I make a joke. Get Mr. P. smiling at least. That's when I hear Caleb's mother in the kitchen. His father says he's gonna go help her make lunch. "If . . . she lets . . . me." He looks at Caleb. "Nobody . . . lets me . . . do anything anymore." Putting his hands on his wheels, he pushes hisself out the room.

Next thing I know, we're in Caleb's car. Not that we talk most of the way to the park. After we get there, he's got plenty to say. Jokes mostly. I think about Maleeka. Is she right about him?

We're at our usual place when I say, "So, what time are we going tomorrow?" He said he'd drive me to Ashley's job around three. And he 100 percent would not cancel on me this time.

"You're paying for gas."

"Cheap."

"I make more money, but it doesn't mean I can spend more money."

I pull out my card. "I could pay for your whole car." I shouldn'tve said it.

We set everything up. I let him go first. Caleb scores with a bullseye. Then two more in a row.

"You been practicing a whole lot, I see?"

"Yeah." That smile is stuck on his face for a while. Mine too. He gets the arrows. Walks 'em over to me. "I shoot early in the morning when the sun comes up. As soon as the birds start singing." It's only him outside then, he says, and a few people going to work. He breathes in deep. Lets it out. "Outside . . . near trees and stuff . . . I feel like . . . like my old self again, not old, you know?"

We're back to doing our thing when he tells me about Maleeka. I just listen. He wants her back, he says. But he knows she's right. "Maybe at the end of the summer . . ." He sits on the picnic table, with his feet on the seat. "I'll take her to a good restaurant. Buy her a necklace . . ." He saw one for three hundred dollars, he says, following a red bird with his eyes.

"Maleeka ain't about the money like that."

He knows, he says. But he's gonna have to do something to get her back.

"Spend time with her," I tell him.

"Like you know."

"I know she thinks you're changing. And she doesn't like it."

He's up, grabbing my bow. Shooting. Talking about bills and his business and Jaxxon being such a good worker. Nothing about the notice on his house.

It just comes out. "They won't put y'all out the house, will they? My dad would lend y'all the money. Just ask."

Caleb aims that thing at me. "Don't you tell your father!"

"Don't you point that at me!"

"Sorry."

How he expect my father not to know anyhow? I ask. The

whole neighborhood probably knows. Not that I say it. I ask about his uncles. Can't they help? Everybody's got money problems, Caleb says, kicking empty water bottles. They all worked for his dad. When he got sick, the business did okay for a while. Then it didn't. Businesses liked working with his father more than anyone else. And his uncles weren't so good at making the business make money.

I ask what they're gonna do now.

He walks over to a tree and sits down. "Last weekend, your dad didn't have any extra work for me," he says. "I mowed lawns all day on Saturday all by myself. All day Sunday too. Four one day. Six the next."

I asked what happened to Jaxxon. He ain't show up, Caleb says. He told Caleb he needed his hair cut. That the grass ruined his sneakers so he had to buy a new pair. "He thought I should help him pay for them. But I didn't."

That's why he was working by hisself yesterday.

"Ain't you tired, working all the time? I would be," I say.

He's getting used to working for my dad, he says. When he's not around, he takes a nap. "Don't tell him. I only do it when I'm in a room or part of a house by myself. And not for long."

"How much time is the bank giving y'all?"

His shoulders go up. "A couple of months." His mother says they usually add more time to it, so maybe they have six months for real, he thinks.

We'll be in school by then. Caleb could be in a shelter or foster care. I stare up at the sun even though it hurts my eyes. "I got an extra bed in my room."

"I have a bed."

"But you never know."

"I know." He walks over and pushes me.

I push him back. "Okay, so you know."

"So, quit treating me like I'm poor."

I push him again. "Okay."

"Okay, then."

I get my stuff and walk home.

CHAPTER 59

I AIN'T THINK he would show up. But a promise is a promise, Caleb said, letting me drive for the first time in a long time. We don't talk all the way there. I don't mind.

Walking back and forth in the ice cream store parking lot, I spray Listerine in my mouth for the last time. I go up to the window and look in. Ashley's in there, alright. On the way here, I rehearsed what I wanted to say to her. Now I can't remember nothing, not a word.

Caleb opens the door. "Just be yourself."

Be myself? That ain't never helped. Not with girls anyhow. I kick a can across the parking lot. Watch it almost hit the back of somebody's ride. Caleb goes in the store. I get a message next. If I don't come in, he's gonna tell her why we're here and how I talk about her day and night.

I practice for five more minutes. Inside, I go to the front of the line. The man Ashley's waiting on ain't happy with me. Neither is anybody else. I try to explain that I just need to speak to her for a minute. She had her head down when I came in. She's looking up now, still scooping chocolate ice cream onto a cone. Smoke from the frozen ice crawls around her fingers, fogs the glass blocking her from us. "John-John." She stands up straight. "That's the line."

My teeth feel dry. I look at the line. Hear people complain about me jumping ahead of them. Lick my teeth. "I only wanted to talk to her for a little while," I tell them.

Ashley tells me to get a ticket. "I can wait on you when I finish with everyone else."

The door opens. The bell rings. Two more people get in line. I get a ticket too and stand in line last. But what if she thinks I'm too short? That's what I'm thinking. What if she thinks my skin is too bumpy? Too dark? Not dark enough? Did she mean what she said? That I should come visit her at work? She don't act like she wants me here.

Nervous, I go use the bathroom. Come back and there's two new people in line ahead of me. Caleb shakes his head. At least the line is moving fast.

Ashley's smiling when it's my turn to be served. "Hi, John." Her voice makes me want to sway.

I order water for my dry teeth, then a triple scoop of ice cream. I get plain old boring vanilla for Caleb. Two scoops. I pay for his and mine, then go give him his cone and come back. "Ashley, wanna go to the movies sometime? Not just with me. I mean . . . You know Maleeka . . . Sure you know Maleeka . . . Everybody knows her . . . even your mother . . . Maybe we could go the four of us anyhow . . . Well, we go to the drive-in . . . If that's too late . . . we can go during the day . . . or to the mall . . . someplace . . . anyplace . . . I know your mother wouldn't want you to be with just me." I bite my ice cream to make myself shut up.

The bell over the door rings. Ashley looks like she's sorry it did. "Welcome to Randy's Ice Cream Parlor." She sounds sad when she says, "John . . . I have to get back to work."

I missed my chance. Blew it. My dad would say it's because I got no swag, no nothing. He's right. "It's okay, Ashley." I get away fast as I can.

I ain't gonna lie to Caleb. Outside, he throws me the key. I get in the car, turn on the engine. Soon as I pull out the parking spot, I stop, almost end up with my head through the windshield. With the car still running and the brakes on, I go back into the store. I feel like running, but I'm walking fast. In front of two customers, I say what I came to say the first time. "Ashley. I'm a nice dude. Your mother would like me if she got to know me. And, well . . ." I tell her what I know about myself for sure. "I would never hit a girl. Never kiss you if you said not to. Never . . . This is my last time asking," I say. "Would you like to go out with me?"

She points the ice cream dipper at a piece of paper on the counter with something written on it.

> Dear John:
> I'm allowed to go to the carnival. Would you like to go with me?
> It's next week.
> Ashley.
> And please don't hold my mother against me.

I grab the paper. Ball it up without thinking. "Yeah. Yeah. I can pick you up. I can pay for everything. What you like to eat? They gonna have rides? I'll pay."

"John. My boss will be here soon."

"Oh. Yeah." I back up. Run to the car. Remember that I didn't ask when the carnival was or where at either.

She ain't forget, I see. "John!" She's at the door holding the ice cream scooper in her hand. "It's Saturday. All day. I can be there at three." She names the street. It's near our old middle school. And please don't text or call her, she says. Her mom checks her phone every day now.

CHAPTER 60

THE CITY GAVE our block money to pay kids to sweep up this summer. It's a grant. Mom wrote the application. Her and her group get to pick and hire the kids themselves. She asked who she should hire? Not Caleb, I tell her. "He thinks he can work sixty-eleven jobs at a time." I mention the streetlight to her. It's out again.

"It's something with the wiring, it turns out," she said. "We're first on the list, they say."

CHAPTER 61

I SHOWER TWICE 'cause today I'm gonna see my girl. Smelling like Dad, I put on brand-new sneakers, looking brand-new from head to toe, my shirt to my underwear to my pants.

Mom takes pictures. Dad asks if I need another twenty. He's already given me a hundred-dollar bill. Carnivals cost a lot of money these days, he told me. "A boy runs out of cash, a smart girl will give him his walking papers."

"That's ridiculous." Mom brushes hairs off the back of my shirt, then walks around me till she's standing in front of me again, next to him. "And don't forget, I paid for our first five dates. You ain't have a dime."

That's why he can advise me about girls, he says. "I was one of them broke-down, sorry brothers. I'm trying to save some man's daughter from the kind of boy I used to be before your mother made a man out of me."

I scratch my head, thinking about all the times he said I should be like him.

Be respectful to Ashley, Mom reminds me. "And don't think you got to be something you ain't. Girls like slow starters too."

"Like Dad?"

He uses his hand like a brush on my pants. "I want you to

be better than me, son." He stands up, staring hard at the bump on my chin. "JJ. Oh, forget it. All the cool in this family went to me."

He's real happy. Could be because I called this morning and told him I was going on a date. I asked if he wanted to come by the house, even though it's not his day. I just wanted him to know I *could* get a girl.

"That girl Ashley," Dad says. "She already knows you ain't smooth, got no playa, got no swag in you. Guess . . . all you can do . . . is . . ." He squeezes my shoulder. Hugs me. "Just be yourself, son."

That's all I wanna be.

Mom touches his forehead. Asks if he's got a fever, is about to die or something. Because he doesn't seem like the same man who called here the other day, she tells him. For a little while, they laugh the way they used to. I leave the house while everything between them is good.

CHAPTER 62

I **KNOW IT** ain't cool, but I do it anyhow. I been doing it since I got here over a hour ago. I turn the stem of my grandfather's watch, twist it back and forth. Put it up to my ear, listen to it tick. I was thinking maybe something was wrong with it. It's not. Ashley just didn't show up.

I start walking, not knowing what to do with myself. Till I see one of the little girls who gets books off us. "John-John!" Jordyn, Char's neighbor, jumps into my arms. "I love my books!" She kisses my cheek.

Her mom looks at me weird like. She don't have to. I was gonna tell Jordie not to jump on me or kiss dudes she don't hardly know. I let her down and go to shake hands with her mom. "I'm the boy that works on the bookmobile, remember?" Since Char left, I've been dropping books by her house.

Jordie's mother don't look like she gonna beat me up now. She shakes my hand. "Oh, you're the one . . ." She smiles at me. "I couldn't get her to read before. Now she's reading under the covers at night when she's supposed to be asleep."

I been back four times since Char left. Leaving different books that I pick myself. Jordie's always at the window, waving. Her grandmother babysits when her mother is at work.

Jordie and her mom go one way. I go the other way. I try to

look cool, walking all by myself, like I don't care about nothing or nobody. When a bunch of girls go by, I turn around and start in their direction, almost tripping. They laugh. That's when I do what my father would do. Ask them if they want company. "I know y'all do." I don't wait for them to answer. "I'm JJ." I go to shake the tallest girl's hand.

They all laugh. But one girl puts her arm through mine. Her other hand goes over my head, like she's measuring how not tall I am. "You cute. But I don't do short."

That's funny to them.

She's pretty. Tall. Mean, I think. "My cousin's your color, not cute at all." Her lips stick out. "But you're cute, Hershey boy."

Her friend says the opposite. But I still wish I was a stone, a rock—I'd throw myself at her. "You ain't cute either." I'm not taking it back neither. "Look at your hair. Who had it before you got it, a rat?"

Right then, Maleeka shows up. She walks up to me, taller than all of us. "Hey, John-John! Come say hi to my mom and meet my stepfather." Her arm goes over my shoulder like I belong to her.

I'm holding her hand when we walk away. "Thanks," I say.

"I can smell mean girls now."

Maleeka's mother is a hugger. Mr. Porter shakes my hand. "So, you're John-John." He says Maleeka talks about me, Char, and Caleb all the time. "Guess y'all be coming to the wedding."

What those girls said is still in my head.

Maleeka tears off a piece of her cotton candy. She sucks her sticky fingers one at a time. "The wedding is in September. Two weeks after school starts," she tells me.

I look to see where they went, wondering if Ashley thinks like them and maybe that's why she treats me the way she do.

Maleeka kisses her mother on the cheek. Hugs him. And says she'll see them later. "Ain't he nice?" she says, when we're leaving.

"He's light." I ain't in a good mood now. "Guess y'all like 'em that way."

She do what all girls do, rolls her eyes. I shoulda kept my mouth shut. 'Cause now she got a attitude.

"Sorry, Maleeka." I pull her into the hot dog line. A ticket gets you a hot dog and a drink for free. I tell her what those girls said.

She pinches more cotton candy. "Well, you said worse to me."

"In middle school."

I change the subject so we don't start arguing. "Are you and Caleb still broke up?"

"We talk, but it's not the same."

Soon as it's my turn, she jumps in line in front of me. "I want everything except onions," she says to the cashier.

We walk and eat. I check my watch a lot, wondering if Ashley's here and why she did what she did to me. After we finish eating, Maleeka says she'll see me later.

"Where you going?"

"I'm working. I came to take pictures." She takes a camera out her backpack.

"Take my picture." I got my arms out. My smile on.

"It's for my newspaper. They didn't hire me. So, I hired myself."

I bend down low. Lean one elbow on my knee. Rest my chin on my fist. Check to see who's looking at me.

Maleeka walks around me in a circle. Gets in close. Bends down low. Turns the lens, the camera, her head, in one direction then another one. Maleeka even lies on the ground and catches me from that angle.

"This is a really good camera." Her mother's fiancé bought it for her, she says. "Me losing the internship wasn't Mr. Porter's fault," she says. But he felt bad. So he got it for her.

Maleeka takes a pencil and a long, skinny notepad out her backpack. She's writing an article about the carnival, other stories about what happens in our neighborhood too, she says, standing straighter, proud of herself. "I'm a very good writer, John-John. They'll see."

"I'm cute. When girls gonna see that?"

"You gotta believe it first."

Thought I did.

Halfway up the street, she asks if I got stood up. I told Caleb about Ashley. He told her, I see. "I guess I did."

"Not me. I don't have a date."

"I can be your date?"

She pushes me, smiling. "Never."

CHAPTER 63

IT FEELS LIKE New Year's Eve out here, only without the snow and cold or guns going off. Everybody's happy. Families are together. We see kids we know kissing and hugging behind buildings and against trees. Mr. Dickerson, who owns two corner stores, is in a wheelchair riding his grandson up the middle of the street.

The neighborhood watch club put the carnival together. Mom's not a part of that. We got booths, games, anything you want. I find another line. Eat two hot sausages and a water ice. Maleeka's over there getting her face painted. When I meet her, she's got tiger stripes on her cheeks.

"Can you believe it?" Maleeka says. "A carnival in our neighborhood. When people read what I write, they'll know."

"Know what?" I say, pinching off her cotton candy.

"How much we like living here." She takes pictures of a boy from my block carrying his brother on his back, and Jelly from art class working the cotton candy stand while fireworks go off and little kids run on the sidewalk with strings of tickets they won on games.

"Hey. Take her picture." It's Jordie in the street about to race. She's carrying an egg on a spoon. She's faster than the other kids. But close to the finish line, she drops her egg and loses. Maleeka keep taking pictures even when she cries and hugs her mom.

"So, you don't like him because he's light-skinned?" Maleeka asks when we start walking again.

"You been thinking about this the whole time?"

She aims her camera at me next, getting in real close. Too close. "Get out of here, Maleeka."

"Why my color and Caleb's color bother you so much?" she wants to know.

I push the camera out my face. And start up the street. Maleeka won't let me get away. She jumps in front of me. Keeps taking my picture, even when I make faces. "It ain't feel good, did it?"

"What you talking about, Maleeka?"

"What those girls said."

I don't answer. Don't stop either.

"You're as dark as I am, John-John. Why you tease me about my skin color in middle school?"

I quit walking 'cause she does. "Don't . . . cry."

People look at me like I hit her or something. I bring up Char and tell Maleeka that I think she treated her way worse than I did.

She's loud when she turns around yelling, "You don't get to say who was worse! I get to say it! Me! Not you! Not Char. Not anybody except me. Me! Me! Me! Because y'all did it to me," she says, pointing to herself.

I feel small, short as the fire hydrant next to us. Worse when she says, "Sometimes, in my dreams I hear you singing that song."

"You never said anything."

"I do when I talk to my therapist."

She finds a parked car to lean against. Takes pictures of nothing really, the ground, the sky. "You started being nice to me only after I came to help you after those boys started beating you up. So I told myself I should forget about how you treated me. Not to make no big deal out of it." But she's back in therapy, she says, now that her mother is remarrying. "We talk about a lot of things, Char and middle school. You. How come you never apologized? Char did. A lot of times."

I thought about apologizing back in middle school. But I stopped singing that song. And I ain't tease her no more. I thought doing that was good enough.

She pulls and picks at her hair. Looks like she's thinking or wanting to say something she ain't sure she should. "Therapy didn't go so good this morning."

They talked about her father, she says. Lately she thinks she's turning her back on him because she loves her stepfather. "I had a good dad, John-John."

I go stand beside her.

"The best." She got the heels of her hands up to her eyes, rubbing. It don't stop the tears. "I was doing real good. Fine with everything. Then—"

"I'm sorry." I can't look at her. "For what I said . . . Sometimes I have a big mouth. I say stupid things. I liked being dark. Then I went to school for first grade and a lot of other kids didn't. I started teasing you so . . . so . . . so I wouldn't get teased, I think." I look over at her, even though I don't want to. "Maleeka."

"Yeah?"

"You got a right to still be mad."

"I'm not still mad."

"Then what are you?"

Sad, she says. "Everything is changing. I don't want my father to think I forgot about him. Char is gone for the summer. Caleb—" He's so busy with his father and making money she didn't know who he was anymore. And even though she's starting her own newspaper, she really wanted the internship. "For a little while I wondered—do they think I'm the wrong color too?"

"I like your color." I mean it. "You the prettiest girl in this neighborhood, at school too."

She turns the camera her way. "I know." Smiles. Takes a bunch of pictures while she makes funny faces.

We both laugh.

Her newspaper will be the best, I tell her. Because we got some good stories here that nobody ever thinks to write about. And only somebody that was born and raised here can tell people what it's like, I say, staring into her eyes.

"You think?" She's smiling, done crying for now.

"Who's smarter than you, Maleeka? Caleb, that's it." I get a little closer and apologize again. "I'm better than I was in middle school, ain't I?"

It takes her a while to say yeah, but at least she says it. "All of us are." She puts her arm through mine. "And Char. She's the most different."

"And if she can change—"

We both say it. "Anybody can."

CHAPTER 64

MALEEKA'S GONE WHEN Ashley's arms come up behind me, hugging me tight. I smelled her before I felt her.

"John McIntyre. Don't be mad."

Yeah, I should be mad, but I'm not. I like how tight and warm Ashley's arms feel. And once I turn around, I get a big hug from the front too.

At the last minute, her mom changed her mind, Ashley tells me. "She didn't know it was in this neighborhood. When I was ready to leave, she told me I couldn't go. It wasn't safe. But I wasn't going to break our date."

Firecrackers go off inside my heart.

CHAPTER 65

I SHOW HER things you got to live around here to know about. Like the school wall painted by elementary kids and teachers tired of all the shooting. There's a double rainbow on one side, and on the other side of the building the sun they painted is always shining. I take her to the basketball court named after the only actor born around here. We stop to hear dudes on the corner freestyling. I don't take her where they be shooting dice, gambling hard. I walk her over to my middle school. They repainted McClenton all white. The inside looks brand-new too. They wanted to change the name, but people from around here wouldn't let 'em.

When Ashley asks if I'm hungry, I rub my stomach. "Yeah. All the time." But I had all the food I want from here. I tell her I know a café nearby. "Café my house."

She look scared.

"My mother won't let anything happen to you."

Let her think about it, she says, walking away. She don't know these streets, I tell her, catching up. "Something might jump out and snatch you."

"Like you?"

I stop under a streetlight. "Yeah. Like me."

She don't move. But a raccoon across the street does. We

watch him take the top off a trash can. Throw it on the ground and jump in. Ashley's running, gone. Laughing. She don't stop until we're at the end of the next block. I ask if she wants to go to my house. This time she says, "Sure."

It's like I'm dreaming. At the same time I'm waiting for my mouth to get me into trouble. Just so it don't, I lock my lips until we get to my house—twenty minutes later. It's like we step out of the sunshine onto the moon, it's so dark on our block.

I hold on to her hand. "Don't let anything happen to me," she says.

"I couldn't go back to school if I did."

I got the front door open, the key in the lock. She's still on the sidewalk. "What's your address?" She needs to let her cousin know where she's at, she says, using her phone for light. It still takes her five minutes to come up the steps.

"Girls first." I step out her way and bow.

"Are you sure your mother's home?"

"Probably. Mom! Hey, Mom!"

My mother's upstairs somewhere when she hollers back. Ashley relaxes some. "Hello, John-John's mother."

Mom laughs. "Hi, Ashley. JJ, you be nice down there."

"I'm always nice."

Dogs follow us into the dining room. Ashley rubs and pets them. I point to a wall full of pictures. I'm in most of 'em. Then there's ones with our whole family, plus my grand-parents, cousins, uncles, and aunts. I show Ashley the table my father made by hand.

"I like the curtains." She walks over and touches them.

"My mother made 'em."

"John, do you have any skills?"

My kissing skills are 100 percent. In my mind anyhow. "I'm nice, Ashley. That's my skill, my superpower."

"I know."

For like three whole minutes, we stare into each other's eyes. The whole time, I'm hoping she don't hear my heart beating, see it through my shirt ready to jump out my chest.

"You can sit at the table, Ashley, or on a stool at the island," I say in the kitchen.

She pulls out the stool at the island. What else is she doing this summer besides working? I say, taking out a pint of ice cream.

"Reading, but I told you that." It's a goal of hers to read sixteen books by the time school begins.

I bring up the bookmobile. "I can bring you some books for free."

Her mother told her she couldn't get any of those. "They're for kids whose parents don't have a lot. It would be like stealing," Ashley says.

I sit three more pints of ice cream on the counter. Butter pecan, chocolate, and vanilla with cherries. Next, I go to the pantry for cones. "Here." I got an ice cream scooper and a jar of sprinkles in my hand by the time I get to her. "Eat as much as you want."

Ashley is greedy. She makes herself a triple scoop, with three different flavors. Covers the whole thing in sprinkles. Every time she licks, they drip like rain. I ain't mad. She made my cone too. Sitting across from her, laughing, is the most fun

I had in a while. Her eyes tear up. She holds her stomach. "Stop, John. Stop."

I'm talking about the time I got beat up. "I swear, Ashley . . . I was praying to Jesus and the devil at the same time."

Spit flies outta her mouth. "You're lying."

"No, I ain't." I jump up. "I seen heaven. I swear I did."

I'm talking about the time Maleeka saved me. I wasn't embarrassed, like people might think, I tell Ashley. I was happy. "Boys my age die all the time. If Maleeka was with the paper back then, she mighta let me die so she could write my obituary."

We both laugh. Ashley uses her long, skinny finger to wipe the table. Pink sprinkles end up on her tongue. She's on her feet when she picks up the paper towels we used, the scooper and stuff.

"You don't have to clean up." I stand up.

"I'm not. I'm helping you."

It don't take long. Not with both of us doing it.

When she came, I thought she'd be gone in five minutes. She's been here a hour and a half. We been together three hours altogether. Mom's been down twice. Once, to introduce herself. The next time just to be nosey, I think. While she was there, I told her to take the dogs up.

In the living room, sitting on the couch, Ashley moves in a little closer. I stare at the wall instead of her, at furniture and pictures and the clock on my cell. Then I get my nerve up and hold her hand. She don't pull away. She squeezes it twice. When her head leans on my shoulder, I'm not sure what to do. Put my arm around her? Let her make the next move?

Respect her boundaries like Miss Saunders and Mr. Young say I should?

Mom makes it easy on both of us. She tells Ashley she might want to head home because it's getting late. "Walk her to the bus stop, JJ. Wait until she boards. Call to make sure she got home safe."

"I know, Mom."

We stand up at the same time. Stare into each other's eyes the way they do in movies. Her mouth is a magnet drawing mine to hers, sticking for a while once they touch. Wish somebody had told me kissing was like this, ice cubes and hot water pouring over your body at the same time, while you falling and floating too. She got to stop me, I like it so much.

CHAPTERS 66

SEEM LIKE CALEB wakes up dusty now, with grass stains on his pants, dirty nails. Mom asked if he smells when he's around me. She saw him at the store. "He be working," I told her the other day. "What you expect?"

But I know what she means. He showers. I been in the house when he's done it. It's always a quick one. He's always in a hurry. Reminds me of my father a little bit, except for the stink. Dad leaves the site clean and fresh as he shows up. Last week, Caleb wore the same shirt three days in a row. Mr. P. finally told him to "take care of that." He wouldn't listen to his mother when she told him.

Sitting on his porch, Caleb yawns, not because I'm boring though. He's tired, trying to hold your eyes open tired. Just got right off of work and about to fall asleep tired, standing up tired. But he's gotta hear the rest of my story, I say. "Because it's a good one." I tell him about yesterday, how the carnival went. I leave Maleeka out. "I think I'll take Ashley to a movie next week."

He warns me not to blow this. To take it slow because a girl like Ashley probably don't talk to boys too often. He thinks I'm lucky to get a chance with her.

"Lucky? She's the one that's lucky."

He starts picking at bandages on his fingers. You get nicked sometimes when you mow. Caleb says he's trying to hire. But if he's got to keep making money, he has to do the work.

Pulling off bandages, he walks over to the trash can. Next thing I know, he takes tens, twenties, fifties out his back pocket. They been in his glove compartment, he says, spreading 'em out on a bench. "Since I started my business."

"Why?"

He don't answer.

Bet there's like six hundred dollars there. Money from mowing lawns, he says. "I only spent twenty dollars of it. Mom's birthday was last week."

I get back to the carnival. "Did I leave out the part about—"

"I'm tired, John-John."

He's about to go in the house when I say, "You know I might spend this, right?" I bring the money over to him, counting it. I was wrong, he's got like nine hundred dollars. "Use the bank. Or your dresser."

His right foot is in the house, his left one's still on the porch when he stops. "You know somebody who wants to do lawns?"

"Not me."

"I pay real good." He mentions making money in the winter. "People hate to shovel snow."

I tell him no. I work hard enough. Mr. Young had me doing inventory the other day and I hated every minute of it. I do ask Caleb about the house. If everything with the bank is the same.

He talks about land his family owns down south. His

uncles are looking into finding someone who wants to buy the trees on the property and use it for lumber. They'll give the money to Mr. P. "That might take forever," Caleb says. "But at least they're trying."

I could post something, I say. People know his father. They would give. That's not the kind of family he comes from, he says.

CHAPTER 67

HE SO TIRED, he let me drive his car to my house. "Don't leave." I get out his car and start running. I get back, and Caleb's in the driver's seat. I drop a box in his lap. After he started working, my father brought him work boots. Dad said he'd take the money out his first pay. He didn't. One day, Caleb asked if he should straight-up pay him back in cash. My father would be offended. "If he wants you to have something, take it," I told him. Dad wanted me to have another pair of new sneakers. There're in the box. How many pairs do I need?

Caleb lifts them out one by one. "My mother wanted me to have these for my birthday, I wouldn't let her spend the money."

"Your mother listens to you like that? My mother wouldn't." I bring up Maleeka. "If you treated her right, I bet she'd still be your girlfriend. And we could double date."

It was a job. Caleb goes off on me. Yelling, he says not to talk about her to him anymore. "In fact—stop talking and lying about girls, period."

"What I do? Why you so mad?"

"They don't like you. When are you going realize that?"

He gets out of the car, telling me even my father knows I can't get a girl. "Everybody at school does too."

He's like a bomb that just blew up in my face. I ain't see it coming or I woulda kept my sneakers for myself. I know things are bad. I know he misses her, I say, but I didn't take her. He messed up, about to mess up with me too, I tell him.

"Stupid . . ." Caleb is looking right at me when he says it.

"Stupid? You're the stupid one . . . thinking you could pay off the house. You in eleventh grade, Caleb. Those bill collectors probably laugh at you every time they hear you talking."

He throws his phone at me.

I duck. Pick it up and throw it at him. "And Ashley does want me!"

He comes after me. I'm backing up, running in between cars on this side of the street, cars on the other side next. But I don't shut up. "Maleeka probably would want me too if she looked around some and wasn't all up under you! Oh, yeah, she's not under you. She got away from you. Good for her."

Mom runs out the house barefooted.

I tell Caleb I'm tired of him always crying about money, looking sad, being broke and begging.

He picks something metal off the ground and throws it at me. That's when Mom gets in between us. "Caleb, I'm surprised at you." Her finger is in his face. "And JJ"—she turns my way—"do not say another word." She moves when I do, blocking me from trying to get to him.

Caleb reaches around her. "You have to beg girls to be with you."

I have to hit him for that. Then I run around Mom and got him in the back. Then the ribs. Mom keeps trying to talk to us. Holding me by the arms, she says to go in the house, now. That's how he hits me in the chest.

"CALEB! GO HOME! NOW!" She's so loud, two windows go up. Neighbors ask if she wants them to call the police.

"No police. Please." She looks at him and me, then takes us by the arms. "You're friends. You shouldn't be out here fighting."

"Here they come. The police!" one of our neighbors yells.

A cop car turns up our street. Mom says to let her handle this. Caleb gets in his car and leaves. Mom sends me in the house and tells me to lock the door. From the window, I watch the police park on our sidewalk and go up to her. She's the block captain, I hear her say. Then she asks for their names. Shakes their hands. Says it was just a minor argument among friends. I call Dad, just in case.

CHAPTER 68

I SHOW UP because I told him I would, last week anyhow. That was the day before we had the fight. Caleb opens the front door. I walk past him like this my house and go upstairs to do what I came to do. I got no funny in me today. Not even for Mr. P. "Ready?" is all I say when I see him.

Maybe Mr. P. is in a mood too. Lying in bed, he don't even look at me or say hello.

"Here's what we need to do." From the foot of his dad's bed, Caleb lifts Mr. P.'s right leg, slow but not too high. "Five stretches on each side in each direction. You do the right one, I'll do the left," he says, like I don't know.

"I know. You okay, Mr. P.?"

He holding and squeezing the bed railings. "What's the fight . . . about?"

We say it at the same time. "Nothing."

Mr. P. faces the wall. He's not his usual self, he says. We can do this next week or the week after, he tells us. "What good is it doing anyway?"

"I got this, Dad."

"I'm here, you know," I say.

"He's my father. You can leave."

I would. But I gave my word to Mr. P. So I shut up 'cause

if I keep talking I'll say something Caleb won't wanna hear. I know that twice Jaxxon took the money he collected and didn't pass it on to Caleb. Char found out and texted me. She got it from some girl who worked at her old day care who got it from Jaxxon, who lives next door to her.

Not paying attention, Caleb pushes his father's leg up too high and too fast.

"Hey, watch it!"

"Sorry, Dad."

"Everybody. Shut up and be quiet! And put my leg down . . . Leave . . . me alone." He closes his eyes like that'll make us go.

"The doctor says if his muscles and movement doesn't improve . . . they'll have to put him in inpatient rehab," Caleb says. "We can't afford it," he says, looking at me.

Mr. P. asks him to please stop talking. That ain't like him. It ain't like Caleb not to do what he tells him. Under his breath, Caleb lowers Mr. P.'s leg onto the bed, slow, like it's a baby he doesn't want to wake up. "It's the truth, Dad."

I sit down in a chair next to the bed. None of my jokes work. Caleb lifts his father's left leg again. He pulls it left. Bends it up and down. Makes it go to the right. Mr. P. bites down on his lip. Balls up his hands. Shakes his head like he's saying no to Caleb or to hisself.

"I have to, Dad."

I stand up. "You know I'm stronger than you, Caleb." I make a muscle. "I'm cuter too. Tell him, Mr. P." I take over for Caleb, mostly for Mr. P. Careful as I can, I work his other leg in all four directions, stopping when he asks me to.

We do his arms next. Massaging his muscles, bending and stretching 'em. Mr. P.'s face stays frowned up like he wants this over with now. They missed three weeks' worth of therapy with his father, so that's why he's so stiff, Caleb says. He had to work. So did his mother. His uncles had other things to do. I bet it's all got to do with the house. They probably have to work even harder to keep it.

Caleb leaves to use the bathroom.

"How's he . . . look to . . . you, John?"

"You know Caleb."

Mr. P. says he knows Caleb is short-tempered these days. That him and his wife have to remind him to shower, to rest, to remember he's just a teenager. He's the one that brings up the note on the door, not me. "I lay here . . . thinking and . . . thinking . . ." Mr. P. says he's got all kinds of ideas for a new business that would bring in money. "But businesses . . . take money." His voice starts to shake like it's cold in here. "And . . . we, we, we need . . . we need money to pay the bank now, so . . . they don't take . . . I . . . can't lose this house."

"Caleb said they were going to sell the trees down south."

He says that'll take too long.

"Maybe my father could . . ."

"No. Not this time."

"Me and Caleb could raise—"

"Don't you hear, no!" He takes my hand and apologizes. Then says he's trying to sell some things.

What they got left to sell?

On the way to the ice cream store that time, Caleb told

me stuff that I never knew. They had to sell a lot of things. It's embarrassing, he said, so he kept it to himself. He sold the chessboard his father bought him. Somebody paid a hundred for it. It was handmade with wood from Australia. The couch in the living room is gone. Sold. His uncles brought in one from their house. He only got seventy-seven dollars for it. So far they've made two thousand six hundred dollars. With Caleb's money, they got five thousand three hundred dollars. They're eleven thousand dollars behind, including fees.

Mr. P. says he doesn't know how it happened. They used to pay ahead. "But once . . . you . . . get . . . sick . . . get . . . behind . . ." He shuts both eyes. "Caleb's not the man . . . of the house . . . I am." He laughs. "Ain't that something . . . A man . . . who can't pay his way . . . can't . . . can't . . . keep a roof over, over his family's head . . . can't stand up without falling down. That a man, John? No."

Caleb comes back with lotion, the good kind, squirting it on his hands, then his dad's legs. Up and down he goes, smearing it on his feet and ankles, between his toes, on his knees and thighs. "Feels good, huh, Dad?"

"Feels good."

Caleb leaves again and comes back with a bowl of warm water and a tub of shampoo.

Mr. P. is embarrassed, I can tell. "I'm supposed to take care of you . . . not the . . . other way around."

I look away when the tears come.

Caleb pulls tissues out the box on the table beside his bed and wipes his dad's face, including the side where the tears roll down onto the bed. "Me and Mom, we don't mind. Nobody minds taking care of you. Okay?" He talks about all that Mr. P. has done for him. Teaching him to read when he was four. Taking the training wheels off his bike the second day he got one. Teaching him to tie a tie, going to every parent-teacher meeting. Teaching him to drive, going on his first airplane ride with him. "And sitting with me in the hospital for ten days when I had strep throat and doctors thought I might die." But even if he never did anything for him, Caleb says, he'd love him anyhow. "You always were a good person, Dad. Everyone knows it."

Mr. P. says he don't know what he did to deserve such a good son, but he's glad he has one. "Glad . . . to have you too, John." Then he makes the kind of joke I would make. "But . . . next . . . time you come, wear de . . . odorant."

"Oh, you got jokes. Not as good as I got."

For the rest of the time I'm there, we joke and laugh until it hurts. Later, Caleb makes lunch. I do the dishes. We don't mention our fight—this one or the other ones either.

CHAPTER 69

I CALLED MY father on the way home and told him everything. "Love you," I said, before I hung up. It just came out.

"Love you too, son."

CHAPTER 70

I'M ON BREAK, sitting on the curb eating a Popsicle with water from the plug rolling in between my toes, over my feet. She's on break too. And I didn't have to call her. She called me. I got so excited, I dropped my phone in the water.

"What are you doing?" That's all she said.

"Nothing." I think about my answer, boring. "Eating lunch." I almost lie and say I'm having a steak sandwich with onions. I ain't lie in middle school, not much. Then I got to high school. Started lying because the truth didn't sound good enough. I wasn't cool. Wasn't like hardly anybody at that school. Except Caleb.

I describe the Popsicle I'm eating to Ashley, the way the water feels on my feet. She asks if I write poetry or something. "Naw, that's Caleb's thing. Maleeka's."

Maybe she's shy. Maybe I am too and just don't know it, but we run out of words, out of things to say. All I hear is water running down the street.

"Ashley—"

"It's my mother."

"Well, she don't know it's me—right?"

"Hi, Mom. No," she says, getting back to me.

"Make something up then. Tell her you're talking to Maleeka."

She mentions Maleeka and her mom's wedding. Her mother don't seem all that interested. In a little while, she's gone.

"That was close." We say it at the same time, laughing.

I got her to myself again. She likes me, she says, whispering.

"I like you too. A lot." I blow her a kiss. It's corny. I know it is. But I wanted to.

She caught it, she says, blowing me one back. Then just like that—she hangs up.

But I don't give her no strikes. We talked for the longest time so far. One hour. Jumping up, I run barefooted to catch up with the bookmobile.

CHAPTER 71

I THINK ABOUT her all the way here, even now with those two women on the bookmobile arguing, looking like they might fight.

"Mr. Young!"

He don't answer. He's up front doing paperwork. Earlier, he said not to disturb him for half an hour. That was a hour ago. But his daughter is sick and his wife keeps calling. I think he's on the phone.

The woman in yellow hollers she had the book first. The one with gray hair in a ponytail won't turn it loose. I yell for Mr. Young again.

"I'm on hold with the doctor. Take care of it, John."

A girl skates over to me. "Can you reach that book, please?" I told her mother I didn't think skates were allowed on the bookmobile, because she might fall. But her mom brought her on the truck anyway, and left her. "Here." I lift her up. "Pick one for yourself." I turn when those ladies get louder. "I read that one at your age," I say, before I put her down. For a minute, I wonder if I did the right thing.

Everybody's watching those women argue, me included. One woman thinks they're gonna start throwing hands. I can't keep my own self from getting beat up. I'm sure not gonna get in the middle of them. I scoot past the girl. Bend down to where we keep books in boxes, behind the racks. What's on the shelves is mostly what we have. But who knows? Maybe there's something else one of 'em wants to read.

I lie. "My teacher read this one." I hold up a book with a man and a woman on the cover hugging. "It's the best book she read all year. She told me that, anyhow." Standing up, I flip through the pages.

The one in yellow turns the other book loose. She takes the book out my hand. It turns out they live on the same block. They both decide to trade books after they read the one in their hands. How come they didn't think about that before I got dust all over my clothes?

CHAPTER 72

WHEN YOU WORK hard, you wanna come home and relax. I walk in the house and what I see? Too many dogs and too many people. Mom's having another meeting. She waves at me but keeps talking. "We need a community center for our kids," she says, "so they don't have to go looking for fun in all the wrong places."

Someone brings up the house parties. The noise. Kids on people's lawns. Beer cans everywhere. I wonder if Mom knows that Dad's friends' kids hold parties like those?

Her group wants volunteers to patrol the neighborhood. If they can get sixteen more people to join, they can start next week, someone says. Mom raises her hand, wish she hadn't.

"JJ, maybe you can tell us what kind of entertainment kids would want in a community center," Miss Effort from across the street says.

"Never mind, I'm good."

"Have you ever been to one of those parties?" someone asks me.

Mom says it for me. "No. He's not that kind of kid."

She tries to fix it, but it's too late. People ask her what she meant by that. I help her out because she's my mom. "I play checkers. Do puzzles. You can't do that at a party."

"Oh, yeah, that's never going to happen at a party around here," someone says. Then I hear someone say they never even seen me with a girl.

They laugh, loud. Mom looks like she feels sorry for me.

Soon as they leave, I call my father. "Dad."

"Yeah."

"Tell me the truth."

"About what?"

"Girls. And don't lie. How many girlfriends did you really have before Mom?"

"A lot."

"Exactly how many?"

"Well, I don't know. I had enough, I know that."

"What?"

"Okay, okay. Three."

"What?"

If he had a son, he says, he promised himself he would not want him to turn out the way he did. "Homeless at eighteen. Couch surfing . . . broke. I wanted you to have fun, to be popular. I wasn't. Not until I was grown anyhow. Now look at me. Everybody knows me. Everybody wants to be me."

"I wanna be myself, Dad."

"Your mom keeps telling me that."

"Well, listen to her."

"Okay."

"Bye."

"Hold up." He asks about Ashley. Says he can see me smiling through the phone when I talk about her. "She good people?"

"I think so."

"You ought to know so, at least by now. It's almost August."

"But how do you know if a girl likes you? I mean, likes you the way you like her?"

He don't got no good answer. He says a man knows, that's all.

I think on that for the rest of the night. I mean, I like her so much. But at the same time, I don't know her well. Not like I know Maleeka and Char. I know them inside and out because we've been in school together for years. Ashley talks about her mom a lot and what she allows her to do and not do. I know more about her mom than her, I think.

CHAPTER 73

CALEB MET ME after work at the bookmobile. He beeped, said for me to hurry up and get in. Soon as I did, Ashley called. I had to get out to talk to her. I know it sounds weird, makes me seem soft, but my toes tingle when I hear her voice. Slow down, I tell myself, only I can't. Better not trust her, I hear Maleeka and Char say. I tell her how much I like her anyway.

When I'm back in the car, I'm still talking to Ashley. I have to take what I can get when I can get it, I say to Caleb. He don't ask questions, just tells me to hurry up with the seat belt. I'm still not buckled in when he drives off.

Ashley says she's got to go, but she don't go nowhere. She likes me whispering in her ear, I think. Caleb ignores us. He drives fast and doesn't answer when I ask where we're going. When he turns into the park, I'm thinking we're here to shoot. But right then, he makes a U-turn. Driving onto the sidewalk near the basketball courts, Caleb stops, gets out and opens his trunk. Raising his voice, he asks if I was coming or not. Like I know why we're here, what he's up to.

It's a accident, me hanging up on her without saying goodbye. But Caleb hollered my name and said he needed help. "With what?" I say, once I get to the back of the car.

"This." He takes out a card table. "And these." Caleb grabs

seven shoeboxes. I take the table. We both set up. He's selling sneakers. Three pairs came from Dad, including the ones on his feet that I gave him.

Dudes watching hoops—instead of playing—start coming. A couple pushing carriages beats them though.

Caleb knows what Jordans are worth. Especially if they've hardly been worn. I think he's asking too much for them. But what one person won't pay, somebody else does. "Look." He lifts up a pair to show the soles to the couple. "Like new. No dirt. Cost me two-fifty. I was always too afraid to wear them."

Quick as my father can pull money out his back pocket, they got cash on the table, walk away with two pairs. Two men leave complaining. They got mad when Caleb wouldn't lower his prices.

Nobody wants the last pair. The sides are faded and they're scuffed at the toe. Caleb gives up on 'em. He sits the box on the ground and folds the table right when another person shows up.

"You don't want those." I pick up the box. And take the sneakers out to show him the problem.

He stares at my feet.

"No."

"How much for those?" He points to the pair Caleb's wearing.

Caleb and me argue when he goes to take 'em off. He never thought I cared one way or the other about what my dad does with his money, he says. Usually, I don't. But this is different. He worries about Caleb. Anyhow, the money Dad spent on those shoes coulda went to me, I say.

Caleb looks at me like he daring me to stop him. Kicking off the right sneaker. Untying the other one, he don't take his eyes off me. He hands over the sneakers, but only after he's paid. I stay where I'm at.

Getting in the car, Caleb tells me I was right. "I couldn't get anyone else to mow lawns. They either have jobs or they laughed when I asked if they wanted to work for me. So I sold the sneakers. What would you do?"

Before I get in the car, I take off my Jordans and sit them on the back seat.

"You don't have to do that," Caleb says.

"Yeah, I do."

At my old high school, it got so bad I went to the gym one day and stood on a chair. Caleb found me before I could do anything. He never told anybody, not even Maleeka.

CHAPTER 74

THEY STOP HIM outside Home Depot like he's a celebrity and ask for his advice about opening up a business. Next thing you know, he's talking about LLCs, why they should incorporate their business. I know 'em. They were in high school when I was in seventh grade. Now they're in college. Lawrence and Jason plan to open a dental practice somewhere around here in a few years. If they drop by sometime, Dad swears he'll give them the name of somebody at his bank who can help them, maybe get them a mortgage, loans, investors, when the time comes. He's smiling. They're smiling. I'm still waiting.

We're inside when my father says for the first time that he wants me to take over the business after college.

"Ah, no. I want something different for my life."

He don't ask what I want. Maybe he don't care, who knows. Pushing the cart, he changes the subject. Says he finally got around to working on his will. Me and his other kids will get all that he and his wife have once they're gone. Mom has a policy on me too.

"Do we have to talk about dying?"

"This ain't about death. It's about money." He rubs his fingers together on both hands. "Everything is about money . . . connections . . . business." He mentions the look on my face.

"How am I looking?"

"Like you don't wanna talk about me dying. So, what do you want to talk about?"

"I don't know."

He brings up Caleb's business. Says as soon as he realizes he needs to connect with more people and go to more functions, it'll take off. "That boy's got a great work ethic. He'll get there."

"Where?"

"Wherever he's trying to go . . . to the millionaires' club, the billionaires' club." Whispering, he says, "I remember, JJ."

"Remember what?"

"Not having money. Sleeping on a mattress on the sidewalk." He starts walking up the aisle.

"I thought you couch surfed."

"Did that and worse."

I take over the cart. End up by the refrigerators, washers, and ovens. He brings up Ashley. I been wanting to talk to him some more about her. Even though I know I shouldn't.

He got too many questions. "Who are her people? What neighborhood is she from? When do we get to meet her, me and my wife?" He stops walking. "Your mother didn't meet her already, did she?"

"Sure she did."

"And?"

"She likes her."

He checks out front-loading washers like he needs one. Opening the doors, closing 'em, he reads the label out loud about the kind of laundry detergent they take. I leave with the cart. Soon as he catches up, I tell him a little bit about Ashley's mother and carnival night and how Ashley came over and had ice cream and met Mom. Be careful around girls like her, he says.

"Don't say nothing bad about her, Dad."

He meant to say girls with mothers like hers, he tells me. He's got his hand on my chin, sort of pinching it, when he says, "Boys got to worry about their reputations too."

McIntyre men got a reputation with the girls, he always told me. Like we had a responsibility to date as many people as we could—ten at a time—if we're able. I remind him he's said that a lot.

"I know what I said." He sits on a plastic chair at the end of the aisle. "Now I'm adding something to it." He scratches his bald head like he ain't sure what he wanna add. "Think before you act around a girl like her. Because sometimes people like her mother see what they wanna see," he says, kicking back, rubbing his bad knee. "And a boy from the hood is just a boy from the hood—worth less than gum under your shoe—to a lot of 'em."

Dad's rubbing his head like he's got a headache when he brings up the will again. "It's been done six months. All I have to do is sign it. Ain't got around to it yet."

I ask if he's scared. Like maybe if he finishes the will something bad will happen to him.

"Could be." He stands up, slow, watching that knee. "Tell me some more," he says, beating me to the cart. Pushing and leaning on it at the same time.

I tell him about one day on the bookmobile when I looked

out for a girl. She was crying because she couldn't remember how to get home. I told Mr. Young I would walk with her until we found her house. And we did—seven blocks away.

"Now, that's what I'm talking about." He slaps me on the back. "You're growing up. A man takes care of women and girls."

Right there in the middle of Home Depot, my father pulls me to him, holding on tight.

"You growing up, boy. Planting seeds. I'm proud of you."

"You are?"

"Why you always acting surprised? I show up for you every time."

I don't say nothing,

"Name a time when I didn't."

"Let it go, Dad."

"Name it."

"When you divorced Mom."

He leaves me with the cart, saying he'll meet me in the car. Taking a wrong turn, he hits his bad knee on the end of a cart somebody left. "JJ, see what you did!"

"That wasn't my fault."

"You can't just have a good day with me. You gotta ruin it."

"Me, I ruined it? No, you ruined it." I push the cart so hard in his direction, he's got to jump out the way not to get ran down.

"Get over here. Now, JJ!"

"How 'bout you stop calling me that?"

"What?"

"John. That's my name."

"Oh, so your little girlfriend calls you by that name?"

"I don't want to be called JJ anymore. If you do, I won't answer."

Under his breath, I hear him say one date and I got some girl running me.

"She run you," I say, still yelling. "Your wife tells you what to do and you do it every time. Especially when it comes to me."

I half expect my father to hit me, he's so mad. I'm mad enough to do something I shouldn't too, I can tell. So I turn around and walk up the aisle, ignoring him with my finger up behind my back.

"JJ! You disrespecting me, boy!"

"Don't. Call. Me. That!" When I turn around, he's sitting in a chair.

"I named you. I'll call you whatever I want."

My eye jumps. "John. That's my name."

"So . . . a million people got that name."

He stands up again, holding on to a shelf filled with door-knobs, and rubs his knee like an old man. At the end of the row, while he's looking, I pull down a box filled with bottles of bleach. They roll everywhere. A manager starts up the aisle. "He'll pay for it," I say, pointing to my dad.

CHAPTER 75

MY FATHER DOESN'T respect me, I tell Mr. P. soon as Caleb lets me in their house. I'm talking so fast his dad makes me repeat some things. Caleb goes downstairs to get me a bottle of water. It was his father's idea.

"Calm . . . down . . ." Mr. P. must've said it to me ten times by now. "Catch . . . your . . . breath."

I'm trying, I tell him. But my father went too far tonight.

Caleb's dad's got this way of making you think everything is going to be alright. His voice seems different tonight. After a while, he don't even talk like a machine.

"Listen, John . . ."

"See. You call me John. That's what I want him to call me."

Mr. P. nods. "Okay. He will. I'm sure."

"You don't know my father. He'll keep calling me JJ out of spite."

Mr. P. wants to know when I finally decided that I needed to be called John.

"Tonight," I say.

"Why . . . tonight?"

"Because it's my name." I slap my chest and tell him everything. Even Mr. P. thinks I had a right to be upset. He says my father was wrong. I mention what I did with my finger. Of course that was inappropriate too, he says. But I had to do something.

I call Mom to let her know where I am. And that I'll be late. Mr. P. wants me to call my father. I can't do that.

Yes, you can, he says. It may not seem fair, he tells me, but if boys don't learn to stop wars, they grow up to be men who start wars.

I don't understand what he just said. Mr. P. can see that on my face, I guess, so he explains. "It's easier . . . for most men to . . . throw money at . . . something. To hit it. Or shoot it. Or kill it. Than to talk . . . about it . . . or talk . . . it . . . through," he says. "Including me."

"No. You're different." Me and Caleb both say it.

He quits talking for so long that Caleb says maybe it's time for me to leave. I'm halfway downstairs when Mr. P. yells, "John! Come . . . back."

In his room, he takes me by the hand. Go see your dad, he says. Don't yell, but say what you got to say to him, he tells me, starting with how my father made me feel at the Home Depot. "That's . . . that's . . . how you . . . stop . . . a war."

CHAPTER 76

I'M ON THE floor, under the window by the radiator in the living room. Mom's on the couch sipping hot tea. Smiling. "He's trying, JJ."

I tell her she can call me John too.

"Okay, John. Guess somebody's growing up, huh?" She kisses me on the cheek.

"Mom. You gotta stop that."

"But you're my . . . ?"

"I'm not your baby, not a boy either."

She changes the subject. Asks about me and Dad. I tell her we had fun the last time we were out. It's easier than rehashing the whole thing. Besides, Dad never called her about it. He left me a message though. He knew the manager because he knows everybody—probably got God's personal phone number. He paid for what I broke and said that he helped pick up. "If it happens again—" I won't repeat his words. Then he said next week was canceled between him and me. "I might not be able to control myself if I see you face-to-face."

I try to get him out my head by asking Mom if she's ready to start school. Next thing I know, I'm walking behind her up the steps with the dogs behind me. In the middle room, she pulls open a drawer. It's a letter from her boss. "She heard I might go to school full-time. So she gave me a raise and said they would pay half my tuition if I made ninety percent or higher in my classes." Mom's hugging me when she says she'll be a supervisor starting next month. "I got all kinds of ideas. Ways we can place older dogs in good homes. People just need a little financial help with caring for them, that's all."

I bring up our dogs and all the new things happening for her. "You think it'll be too much, Mom?"

She asks if I ever felt slighted or less loved since their divorce. I tell her no. If I do, Mom says, let her know and we'll change a few things.

If she could go back, would she not marry my father? I ask. "And don't say you would because he helped make me. Just answer the question."

Mom wants to know if there's something going on between my father and me that she should know about. "Because now that I think about it . . . you've been a little quiet the last few days. Sorta sad." She rubs my cheek. "Or did you and Caleb fight again?"

I used to tell her everything. I got to pick and choose what I share now. I mean, I ain't no kid. And sometimes she breaks her promises. She'll tell Dad what she swore to me she wouldn't. Truth is, your mom ain't your girlfriend. Char said it to me the other night. "Keep some things private even from her, JJ. It ain't her job to fix every problem you got."

Maleeka agreed. Then when they started talking about this boy Char met, I got off the phone.

"I'm cool, Mom. For real."

"You will always be my baby."

I ask her not to say that.

"What am I supposed to call you, my little man?"

Since I last saw my father, I been thinking about my nickname. People been calling me JJ or John-John since I was born. Heading for the door, I tell her what I told Dad. "Call me John."

"Since when?"

"Ain't that what you named me, Mom?"

"Well, yeah . . . John. We did . . . We sure did."

CHAPTER 77

I CAME TO his cookout anyway. Mr. P. thought I should, Caleb too. And don't go angry, Mr. P. said, or the war between me and my father won't stop. He had a good point. But I'm here because me and Dad had a talk too. Last night. Late, late late. I called him to apologize for my part. My father apologized too. He said he didn't want both of us at the party with our lips stuck out. "And maybe . . . I did say some things I shouldn't. But JJ . . . John . . . whoever you are these days, if you destroy someone's property again . . . I swear, I'll call the police on you myself."

Caleb says he wouldn't. I don't think he would, but with my father, you never know.

Dad is the best dressed one here, besides his wife. With a beer in his hand, he fist-bumps Caleb, stares at his work boots, but don't say a word. He winks at me. "You good, John?"

"I'm good."

"Then come on. There's people I want you to meet."

Looks like about fifty people here. The music's loud, kids are everywhere, and there's plenty of tables with food on them, no grills though. He did the grilling six this morning, he tells us. "She brought in caterers for everything else," Dad says with his back to us. "'Cause nobody can do barbecue better than your old man."

Dad stops just about every minute to introduce us to somebody. To talk with people who work for him or used to. We three are near a tent when he brings up Jackal, the one Caleb saw stealing. "I fired him." Dad slows down and walks beside me. "Not sure how come I never noticed what he was up to." He asks Caleb if he ever saw anything.

"No." Caleb cuts his eyes at me.

Next time his workers don't speak up, Dad says, they're all fired.

"Well, that's not right," I say.

"Can't have my profits walking out the door or people around who don't look out for me the way I look out for them. Understood?" He looks at Caleb.

"Yes, sir." Caleb reaches back to scratch his neck. "It won't happen again, sir."

Me and Dad both look at him.

Stopping, my father asks Caleb if he's saving the sneakers he gave him for a rainy day. Dad checks out his work boots. "'Cause far as I can see it's raining pretty hard."

Caleb and me look up. The sun is hot and it ain't rained in weeks. "Oh, I know what you mean, Dad."

When Caleb says he's saving his sneakers for the first day of school, I keep quiet.

"Good idea." My father squeezes his shoulder. "Hope you're spending some of your hard-earned money on yourself."

"My parents need it more than I do."

If he's not careful, Dad tells Caleb, he'll resent them. "And feel like they stole your childhood, by making you work your life away."

I'm surprised to hear him say it.

"You work hard . . . enjoy some of what you make, boy." Soon as Dad sees one of his friends, he forgets about us. "Yo, Dae-Dae. Hold up." Just like that, him and his foreman go find a dominoes game to sit in on.

Caleb gets a call from Maleeka. I ask if they're back together. He wrote her a poem, he says. Three. "Hope they work."

"You still love her?"

"I never stopped."

"Good luck."

Next thing I know he's under a tree with his back to everybody. That's when Giovanni comes over to me, sitting on my feet like I'm a stool. He squeezes my legs with his arms. Says I'm a zombie. For me to stick my arms out and talk and walk like one.

Sweat from my face drips down on him. He growls. I growl too, then lift him up and sit him on my shoulders after he asks. I almost said no. But he's good at getting you to do what you don't want, just like my father.

"I'm a airplane." Giovanni sticks his arms out. "Fly me over there." I fly him over to the swings, past the water fountain, under the bridge. I figure I'll get it all over with at one time, so I can enjoy myself later. But after he sees his mom, he wants down.

"I'm glad you came, John-John," she says, holding him and rubbing her stomach.

"John. That's my name."

"I thought you said call you . . . oh, never mind. Glad to

see you, John. Come by the house sometime. Your father and your brother miss you."

Something about her always makes me mad. "You said I wasn't allowed in."

"I never said that, JJ . . . um . . . John-John."

"Don't call me that! My name is John; it's always been J-O-H-N, John!"

She puts Giovanni down. "Okay, then!" She wipes sweat off her forehead, then dries her fingers on white shorts that match Dad's. "You're invited to the house tomorrow for Sunday dinner, if you want to come."

"You changed the rules? Because before you said—"

Whatever she said about me not coming by the house ain't how she feels now. She changed her mind, she says, doing that rubbing thing again. She turned forty-four a couple months ago and she's getting too old to hold grudges, she tells me. "Plus, we have another one coming." She moves closer. "Girls need their brothers. And you're her big brother."

"You're my big brother too, right?" Giovanni hugs my legs.

"Yeah, right."

His mother is slow reaching for my hand. It's almost on her stomach when she says, "Don't worry. You can't hurt her."

She's taller than Dad and me. Mom is taller than us too. Looking up at her, I don't say nothing.

"Your mother and Big John—"

I try to pull my hand away. She don't let me.

"Sometimes, I wish they hated each other. It would be easier."

I never thought about it being hard for her to be married to my father. But it was hard for Mom too, at least she says so. "He works day and night," Mom would say. "Knows everybody, helps everyone, can't be still for a second." It was exhausting, she told me once. "But he's loyal," she said. "And no one can deny it."

"I don't have any more fight left in me, John-John. I mean, John."

Dad jumps up yelling about how good he is at dominoes. "Now, who here wants to embarrass themselves trying to win against me, once I take these people for all the money they got?"

His wife is laughing when she says, "He can't help it."

"Nope, sure can't."

Giovanni leaves and comes back with ice cream. Sheila wipes it off his nose. Gives him a kiss on the lips. I gotta go, I say. She takes ahold of my hand, keeping me where I am. It's not easy, being somebody Big John loves, she tells me. "But it's worth it."

Dad's waving at her, yelling real loud how good her mac and cheese is and why everybody ought to get some before he eats it all up.

"See."

For the first time, I bring up the baby. "He'll spoil her."

"Shouldn't he?" Sheila brings up Mom. Once the baby comes, she's hoping we can all be—not friends—but not the way we are now, she says. "Maybe like good neighbors."

"They used to argue a lot." I pick a ladybug out my hair. "Still do . . . sometimes."

"He ain't easy." She gives me one of those almost smiles.

"Nope. He ain't."

"But he loves you." She lets my hand go. "And me. And them." Patting her belly, she says, "I'm not going nowhere, John. I'm here for good."

"Me too."

Sunday is baked chicken and lasagna day at their house. I'm invited, she says. "Just come." I don't have to call beforehand or nothing, she tells me.

Right then, Giovanni attacks my legs, grabbing 'em from behind. I end up on the ground with him, wrestling. Dad runs over, taking a million pictures. Somebody gets the idea to take one of our whole family. I wanna say, we ain't exactly family, but some of my uncles and cousins end up in the picture too. Plus, I can hear my mother saying, "He's trying, JJ . . . Her too."

CHAPTER 78

FEELS LIKE I'M at a funeral, mine. Ashley came by a little while ago, without texting or calling. Her cousin drove her. She's in the car over there. At first I was happy to see her, now I ain't. I think she's quitting me and we aren't even a couple yet.

Ashley bends down and hugs our dogs hard as I wish she'd hug me. What she whispers in Esmerelda's ear, I'll never know. But they both look like they feel sorry for me now.

Nothing I can say is gonna change her mind, Ashley says. But then out of nowhere, she hugs me too. I don't hug back because I ain't sure I'm supposed to. But when she don't let go, my arms naturally go around her waist. I sniff her hair, hear her say that I should find another girl to like. "Because you're a nice boy and you deserve somebody nice."

"You're nice."

"Yeah, but my mother isn't. What she says about boys from around here . . . me and my father, we say she shouldn't, but it's what she thinks."

"What do you think, Ashley?"

"Me? I wish I had a different mother. But this is the mother I have."

I remind her about what she said earlier in the summer, about doing what she wants to do and not always following her mother's orders. "So, is this what you wanna do?" I didn't want to ask the question, but I had to.

She's talking about her mom again. Her brother and sister too. But she don't say anything else about us, or me. I joined book club to meet girls. To get a girlfriend. I'm close, but close ain't good enough, Dad would say. "I should go, Ashley."

"I'm sorry."

"Girls always say that to me."

"I really am."

I go in the house and slam the door.

CHAPTER 79

CALEB'S IN A BAD MOOD. Me too. We both got our reasons. He ain't have to ask what was wrong with me after he came into our house. He knows me like I know they lost the house, not that I figured it would happen the way it did. Mr. P. sold it.

Dad told me a couple a days ago what happened. I didn't reach out to Caleb because I ain't wanna feel worse than I already do. What Ashley did at my house broke my heart.

"I almost had it paid up," Caleb says, sitting over there on my bed.

That's not true. Dad thinks Mr. P. did the right thing. This way they can pay what's owed from the sale of the house and maybe have enough money left over for a down payment on an apartment, my father said the other day.

"He was only thinking about himself." Caleb's right leg won't stay still. The knuckle cracking and popping don't stop either. "He went behind my back. That's not him. We talk about things. That's our family. I'll never trust my father again."

Caleb don't mean it. He's got the best father, one of the good ones. Mr. P. being sick and Caleb thinking he was the man of the house was a disaster waiting to happen, Dad said yesterday. "But they'll make it through."

Like Dad, Mom thinks selling the house might be the best thing for them. "Houses around here sell for a lot of money. If their family lost theirs, it would be like throwing money out the window," Mom told me.

Mr. P. told Caleb they might make an extra eighteen thousand dollars when it's all done. Enough to get a three-bedroom apartment for six months. He looks at me. "In a different neighborhood."

That ain't Mr. P. He loves it here as much as I do. But what's done is done. Like me and Ashley. "I need a new girlfriend, quick."

"You never had one."

"Well . . . I need one anyhow." I finally tell him about Ashley. "You think I should go to school and talk to her mom? She works summers."

"Forget about her. Or you might end up like me."

"Maleeka might still be your girlfriend, if you try harder."

He's back to talking about the house. "I should have kept my money. You saw my tires? Almost bald." He lifts his foot. "I've been wearing these hard boots most of the summer. I keep blisters on my feet." He brings up all the things they sold, couches and toasters, his grandmother's chest. "If I knew Dad was going to sell the house—"

"You woulda tried to stop him."

"Yeah."

"Guess that's why he didn't tell anybody."

"I had a right to know. I paid the bills. I took care of him."

"Well, your mother and uncles helped."

He turns red in the face and walks over to the door. "Let's go. And I don't care where."

"You sure?"

"I said I didn't care."

I open the top drawer to my dresser. "Here." He don't catch the washcloth I throw at him. "Sorry." I got two boxes of soap when I get to him. "Mom keeps new toothbrushes in her bathroom."

We wash. Brush. Spray on cologne. At the mirror, I brush my hair and add some waves. Caleb's in the kitchen when I get downstairs. Mom knows not to bring up his father.

Dad got a call from Mr. P. the day before he found a buyer for the house. He said he fell down in his bedroom. He had to crawl to his phone to call my father. Dad told me not to mention any of this to Caleb. "Could you help me?" Mr. P. said to Dad. "Are you near the house?" He said he didn't want to bother his wife or his brothers. They do so much for him, he told Dad. Caleb was at work. Plus, Mr. P. wasn't supposed to take a shower by hisself anyhow. But he wanted to be his old self again, he told my father. To get dressed by himself. Walk outside by himself. Drive his car around the corner at least.

Even though Dad said for me not to tell Mom, I told her. She cried. Maybe that's why Mr. P. sold the house, she told me. "It was something he could do without anyone's help or permission."

Mr. P. never put his wife's name on the house, Dad found out. He sold it to the first person who made an offer. Caleb said his mother is talking about getting a divorce.

In the living room, Mom brings up Caleb's mother. I sit down on the couch. Caleb can't keep still.

"I saw your mother the other day at Safe Food, the grocery store," Mom says. "Tell her if there's anything I can do—"

He cuts her off. "We're good. Thanks."

I get up to open the door. She asks where we're going. "Nowhere," I say. Which is sort of true.

Mom tells me to be home by ten. I step outside. "It's nine. Stop treating me like a baby."

"Watch your mouth!" she says, walking behind me.

"Can't I have a different curfew this time? Eleven thirty."

I'm looking at her. She's thinking, I can tell. "Caleb . . . needs some fun," I say. "Tell her, Caleb."

He's on the sidewalk. "Mrs. McIntyre."

"Yes."

"You know my father, right?"

"Yeah."

"Why would he do it?"

"We parents do the best we can, Caleb."

"He shoulda set it on fire. It's not going to be ours anyhow."

Mom's got no words, I can tell. She gives me a later curfew though. "But if you break it—"

"I won't."

I need to let her know where we end up, she says, following us to the car. "And y'all be careful." Then she says I can thank my father for this. "He's been bothering me about your curfew."

Mom texts me and says she's letting Caleb's mother know we're going out and he's not doing so good. *Watch him*, she says.

CHAPTER 80

I TELL CALEB we're not talking about his father, their house, or Ashley for the rest of the night.

"I'm homeless. Not talking about it won't change it."

"No, you're not."

"Then what's my new address?" He opens the trunk and throws in his backpack.

"You been using my stuff?"

He takes out the case and unzips it. "Yeah. I lost some." He zips up, unzips his backpack. "I never did get the rest of it to the bank."

"Why?"

"I liked counting it. Looking at it get bigger and bigger. I wanted to dump it on my dad's bed one day and say let's go to the bank and pay off the house." He closes the trunk. Says he'll put the money in the bank on Monday. "Where do you want to go?"

I'm hungry. Wishing I had a steak hoagie with plenty of onions and peppers. He wouldn't want to go eat though. "We can go anyplace you want."

"You really must feel sorry for me."

His life is screwed up enough, so I keep Ashley and her mother to myself. But I let him know we not talking about girlfriends either, not tonight. Anyhow, Maleeka's got her own problems. The wedding got pushed back. She told me today, not him. "I can drive," I say, even though my license says I can't drive after dark.

He'd let me if it wasn't a Saturday night, Caleb says, getting in. "Because anything bad that's ever happened to us, happened on a Saturday night."

"You right."

The cops stopped us once. Another time, I was doing sixty-five in a construction zone. The car spun and skidded across three lanes. Only thing that saved us was the guardrail. And Dad. We called him. He got us a tow truck. Talked to some of his police friends and some dudes he knows in city hall. I got a four-hundred-dollar ticket, and that's all. Dad paid to get the car fixed. Luckily, no other cars were around.

We're off the block when I start naming places we should go. He ain't interested in none of them. It's like this for a while, him driving, us getting nowhere. At least there's girls out here. Plenty. Cute. On every block. Looking like they want somebody. I want somebody. Ashley was supposed to be my somebody. Now she's not.

My father always said the best way to get over one girl is to find another one. I lean out the window, waving, hollering. Some of 'em smile. Some are just plain rude. I try to get Ashley out of my mind, but I can't, like he can't stop talking about their house. "Grown-ups ruin everything," I say.

Caleb beeps and stays on the horn a long time. Even though the person crossing the street is in a wheelchair with grocery bags hanging off the handles.

"Dude," I tell him, "you know you wrong."

Maybe tonight he wants to be wrong, Caleb says. Maybe tonight he wants to do something bad, he tells me, speeding through a red light, the next one too. When he stops, I got to hold on to the dashboard not to get thrown out the car.

He drives slow for a long time 'cause maybe he scared hisself. I know he scared me. I keep checking my seat belt and looking at girls so pretty it ought to be against the law. I whistle. Stick my tongue out. "See, I told you he ain't no good," I can hear Ashley's mother say.

I get good grades. I got four thousand dollars in the bank. I never been kissed before I met Ashley. Why her mother think she's too good for me?

"I hate him."

"No, you don't, Caleb."

He slams on the brakes, just missing the car in front of us. I take off my seat belt. Open the door. Walk around to his side, yelling, "If you wanna die, die! But you ain't gonna kill me!"

He's driving again when he says, "I only bought myself one thing this summer. My mother said we had to sacrifice. I sacrificed fun, my money, time with Maleeka, studying for the SATs," he says, driving like he normally does, like an old lady. "I wasted my summer, my money, everything."

"We both wasted our summer."

CHAPTER 81

WHEN CALEB STOPS the next time, it's because I tell him to. There's a party going on Richard Road. I only know because of the sign out front with Mr. Junior's sons' names on it. THIS IS A TWINS PLUS ONE PRODUCTION, it says.

Dad's always talking about them and their parties. Time for us to see what my father wants me to see, what Mom and her block club doesn't.

Inside is so crowded, I can hardly see where I'm walking. So hot and sweaty, underarms that need shaving drip sweat. My eyes don't stay still. They go from one girl to the next, looking 'em up and down, watching 'em come and go.

Caleb ends up standing by the wall looking sad. Not me. I go where *they* are, the pretty ones. The tall, thick ones. They're all in the middle of the room, waiting for me. I tell myself that anyhow. I don't ask to dance. I go up to the first one and start dancing. She can't help herself, I'm good and not scared for once. Maybe 'cause of Ashley's mean mother or because this is my neighborhood, my zip code, and people who don't mind being around people like me.

T-One walks up to me and says his father told him that my father said he'd get me to one of their parties one day. "I don't think you can take the smoke though." He asks who I'm here with.

"Caleb."

"The yellow dude with the yellow convertible?"

"That's him."

"Sweet," he says, walking away.

He don't stick around long. No worries, I ain't come to talk to no dudes. The next girl I dance with asks if I came by myself. Her name is Bailey. She looks like a Bailey.

"No," I say. I point to Caleb.

Bailey whispers in my ear with her hands up to her lips. There's another party going on, she tells me. Better than this one. And her friend is there waiting. She looks down at her high-heeled boots. They brand-new. She can't walk far in them, she says, bending over, unzipping one, taking it off in the middle of the dance floor. "Please."

"No," Caleb says when I tell him about her.

"But she needs us." I look in between people on the floor and find Bailey again. "And she's a girl." I finally tell him about Ashley's mother.

He starts walking, zigzagging between people dancing close and crazy fast on the floor. I catch up to him. It don't take us long to find Bailey and leave.

CHAPTER 82

SHE AIN'T TELL us she had to make a stop. We're cool with it though. Till the police show up. "Move or get ticketed." He shines a flashlight in Caleb's face, at our hands, into my eyes.

I stretch my arms out. Put my hands on the dashboard. Caleb's driver's license gets handed over because the police officer asked him for it. Caleb's hands would normally go on the dashboard like mine while the cop checks him out, because that's what our fathers taught us we should do, but tonight Caleb ain't up for that. He folds his arms. Gets loud. "We didn't do anything! All he had to say was move your car! In other neighborhoods they get treated differently." Caleb stares back at the police car, sees the lights flashing. "If Bailey wasn't in the store, I would drive away."

"Shut up, Caleb. I wanna go home tonight. Not to jail."

"Jail. Home. Homeless. They're all the same." His lips start shaking. Snot and tears come at the same time. Only he don't move to wipe 'em away or put his hands where they should be.

"Caleb, every day my father does something stupid. Your father's different, he mostly gets it right."

"I used to think he did. I thought he was perfect . . ." He turns so I can't see him crying. "The best father in the neighborhood."

"He's still better than most."

"No, he's not."

People don't notice kids like us unless we're in trouble. The cop gives Caleb his license back, doesn't notice that his face is wet. He does let us know there's parking around the corner, plenty. He says for us to have a good night. But you can't once you been stopped by somebody carrying a gun.

That cop was right though. There's lots of parking around here. Not one sign saying they give out tickets if you stay too long. I'm thirsty, so I get out the car. Open the trunk. Drink a bottle of water, warm. I walk one over to Caleb. "Here . . . for you." And hand him some napkins too.

Then it happens. What our mothers and fathers always warn us about. Not watching my surroundings, I let some dude walk up behind me. "Put your hands up." If he got to repeat it, I won't like it, he tells me.

I raise my arms. Caleb too.

He's tall. I'm gonna remember that. With thick, ashy, hot sausage fingers, skin the color of cashews. I can't see his face.

His hands go in my back pockets, then the front ones. His friend takes my phone. I left it on the seat.

I notice his boots. The kind men who work with my father wear. Dirty. Hard. Steel-toed boots. "You know my dad?" I wanna ask. I know better.

Caleb gets out quick because they tell him to. He hands over his wallet and phone. Next thing we know, they're in his car, driving away with my stuff and all that money in his backpack. Before they get too far, they stop. Back up. Pointing to me, the one who ain't driving says, "You related to somebody?"

"Huh?"

The driver guns the engine. "You stupid? Can't hear?" Opening the door, he says he can make me hear.

My hands go up again. "I ain't nobody."

"Me either." Caleb don't hold up his arms. "We go to school, that's all. We were at a party. That's all. A girl is waiting for us to take her home."

It's true what they say. You feel like wetting yourself when something like this happens. Soon as they're gone, we find bushes in front somebody's house. It feels like we'll be there all night.

CHAPTER 83

IT'S LIKE CALEB'S got a rock in his hand when he hits me in the head. Before I know it, I'm down on the ground being punched and kicked in the chest and ribs. He's been wanting to beat the whole world up all this time, seems like, but all he's got is me.

He blames me for everything. Says he worked and saved three summers for his car. I tell him those dudes stole from me too. Holding me down on the ground, he talks about his money, his father, hating his life too. I don't know how I get up, but I do. I come up swinging. And get a few good hits in, just like him. "I told you to take it to the bank!" I say.

"It's my money." He punches me in the chest. My whole body vibrates. "I can do what I want with it."

"Well, now it's gone."

Caleb calls me immature, irresponsible, stupid.

"I'm glad your car is gone. And your house."

That does it. With a punch that feels like a desk hit my face, he knocks my front tooth out, splits my bottom lip, and busts my nose. For a minute, I stand there bleeding everywhere. Then I run home.

CHAPTER 84

MY MOTHER CAN'T figure out which way to go. She opens the freezer. Takes out a frozen bag of peas. Runs past me out the kitchen to get her phone. Comes back saying, "I think your nose may be broken."

It swelled up. It's hard for me to breathe.

"Who did this to you?" She sticks the frozen bag in my hand. "Lean your head back. Not like that." She does it for me, pushes my head back. Lays the cold peas on my nose and face. "I'm calling your dad."

"I'm awright."

She wanted to call him and the police as soon as she saw me. I begged her not to. I lied and told Mom I said the wrong thing to somebody's girlfriend and he ain't like it. I'm not bleeding so much now, mostly I'm swollen, with dried blood everywhere and cotton stuck up my nose.

"Have you seen yourself?" Pulling me up from the chair, out the kitchen, through the dining room, Mom stands beside me in front the long mirror in the living room. She calls my father next. "We need a ride to the emergency room . . . right now. Your son . . ." She goes for more peas. "Here. Your dad will be out front in five minutes. Get your phone." I tell her I don't know where it is. She gets her purse off the hook on the back of the closet door and walks with me to the front door.

Hospitals don't rush just because you're ruining their seats and floors or your dad keeps hollering for them to hurry up and wait on you while your mother cries at the front desk. They act like it's any ordinary day because to them it is. To me, it's just how my summer's been going. Terrible.

We're all here, including Giovanni and his mom. Maybe because it's late and they couldn't get a babysitter. Giovanni cried when he first saw me. I had to tell him I was okay, fine.

Sheila, Dad's wife, is holding a row of seats for us. In the back seat of the car, she held on to my hand. I ain't mind. Giovanni only stopped crying once she did, then he got me to agree to come to the playhouse in the yard when I get better.

At the front desk, Mom gives the nurse more information about me. My age. Insurance stuff. Why I'm here. Dad asks if I won at least.

"No." Anyone can tell I didn't, so why lie?

"You shoulda."

I lift the bag of peas. "Next time, I will."

"Next time?" He shakes his head. "Maybe you and I need to find out who did this so you can finish it—tonight."

Sheila and Mom ask him to be quiet. "Anyhow, as long as he did his best." That's Mom.

"Fighting never solved anything." His wife does that rubbing thing.

The world is in a mess because of thinking like that, Dad tells them. He rubs his forehead like he's got a headache. Moving too much in his seat, he tells me and them that I'd better figure out a new way to handle myself because this way ain't working. "Don't you get tired of losing?" At least he whispered it.

I find myself a seat near the TV. Maybe they crashed Caleb's car. Or robbed somebody else and got caught. The news will report it if they did.

My father finds me. He brings up the fight again. Do I plan on losing for the rest of my life? he asks.

Mom asks how come he don't know I could get shot or killed out there. He reaches for a newspaper sitting on a table in the middle of the room. He opens it like he's reading when we know he ain't. "You and Caleb. Boys like y'all can't let people get away with nothing. Otherwise, they'll come for you again and again until—"

I try to talk. He won't let me. A man's got to handle his business, my father says. He hopes I'm handling mine. Then he asks if maybe I need boxing lessons.

"No!!! And I don't wanna keep talking about it."

He looks down at me. "Some things worth fighting for, boy."

I swallow hard. "I lost, okay? Sometimes you lose."

"But you ain't always supposed to lose."

CHAPTER 85

MOM MADE ME call Mr. Young, then Miss Saunders. I had a accident, is all I told 'em. I'd be missing a week of work, I said. I don't want them knowing my business. Plus, I can't show up with a mouth full of stitches and bruises, a bottom lip big as a biscuit. They had to sew up the hole where my tooth was and my inside lip where I bit it. I'll get an implant in a few weeks.

"I hope your good time was worth it," Mom said a little while ago. Then she brought up my phone. "Where is it again?" Mom asks for like the hundredth time.

I lie. "I think I lost it while we were fighting."

Tomorrow she wants me to get a new one. And pay for it myself. That'll teach me, she thinks.

"Teach me what?"

"Not to lie." She frowns. "You're leaving something out about that fight. A whole bunch." If Caleb's family and him wasn't going through such a hard time, she'd call and talk to him about it, she says. "Poor thing."

CHAPTER 86

I WOULD BE embarrassed for Ashley to see me like this. But Maleeka saw me get beat up once before. She came with a broom, swinging it. Nobody would believe it because she was bullied all the time at school by me and Char. Turned out she wasn't a punk after all. I had respect for her from then on. Dreamt about her sometimes. Wished she was mine even when she was his. But she's gonna always be his and look out for him first.

"Caleb ain't a fighter. You either. So what y'all fight about? And what happened to his car? He needs it."

"Can we please not talk about him?"

Sitting on the steps of my house, I stretch my legs out. Roll my head in a circle to relax my neck. "It's just something between me and him. Nobody else needs to know about it."

Maleeka says we all have too many secrets already. She gets up to sit next to me. With one eye closed and her lips twisted like I stink, Maleeka says she thinks I'll need new stitches. Handing me another tissue, she asks who I'll fight next. "Me? Char?" She brings up the boys in our neighborhood. "Everybody's mad. Hitting, fighting, killing. I'm tired of it. We all are."

"It ain't everybody."

"Seems like it to me."

"We got our reasons."

"That's what the KKK says."

She's reading a book on the Klan. "To them, there is always a good reason to kill us. People can justify whatever they want."

Who was talking about them? Some boys around here wouldn't know who they were if you asked 'em. But, if they showed up, we'd be ready for 'em. She brings up the obituaries she writes for her newspaper. She's so tired of doing 'em, she could scream. "And not just because they're boring. But because it's sad. And I know some of the boys and they're . . . us."

"Boys fight in other neighborhoods," I tell her. "Asians, white boys, Latinos. All over the world. It's just what we do."

"But I live here, so this is the neighborhood I'm concerned about." Maleeka puts her arm through mine, her head on my shoulder, and I melt inside. "I don't want anything bad to happen to you or Caleb."

"It won't."

"Yeah, it will. I can tell."

"Maleeka?"

"Yes?"

"Never mind."

"Ask me."

"Never mind." I'm about to stand up when she asks me again what's wrong.

The same thing that was wrong last spring, I wanna say. That's been wrong all summer. Somebody like her wouldn't understand. Only other boys like me who keep losing would know how I feel. Back at school, people gonna talk about their trips and parties, their new outfits and what them and their friends did or what some girl did for them. What I got? Nothing but a busted lip, a missing tooth, and stories about a girl who was almost my girlfriend. Even Caleb's got more than that.

She pulls out her camera. Starts going through pictures. "Maybe I should write about y'all." In black and white, I see Char, her, and me, houses on our block, kids standing in front the fire hydrant getting soaking wet. For the first time, I notice her perfume. It's the same smell that stays in Caleb's ride.

I stand up. "I need to go. See you later." I walk up my steps, then come back. "Come on. I'll walk you home."

Girls can get you to do anything. Maleeka gets me to take the long way to her house. "Make up with him," she whispers. "For me. Please."

"I can't do it, Maleeka."

"Why?"

"Because it's not what we do." My father is right about some things; we ain't the same as girls.

Maleeka brings my mom into it. How am I gonna protect her if I keep getting myself into fights? she says. "Somebody might come for her to get to you."

"Not your boyfriend."

I'm right about that, she says. But that don't make her wrong about everything else, Maleeka tells me. "Like Ashley. This is all because of her, I bet." She don't wait for an answer. Just tells me to quit being a idiot. Because this won't be the first or the last girl not to like me or want me. "You can't be mad at the whole world or hurting people because you didn't get what you wanted, John-John McIntyre."

"But I never get what I want! And call me John!"

"What?"

I give up. She don't understand. So, for a little while I focus on the sirens and birds, an argument up the street, her breathing soft. "I used to like you, you know. A lot."

"I know. But Caleb was always the one for me."

"I know."

"Anyhow, you got over me, didn't you?" Maleeka asks.

"Pretty much."

She punches my arm.

I lie. "Okay, I did. By eighth grade."

Well, I'll get over Ashley too, she thinks. "And end up dating lots of other girls. You a nice boy."

"EVERYBODY, STOP SAYING THAT!"

"You didn't use to be. But you are now. And one day those girls will see it."

Caleb's lucky, even if he thinks he isn't. Even if he don't ever find his car. Whispering, I ask Maleeka not to move, no matter what. "Now, close your eyes." I go stand in front of her.

"John-John—um, John . . ."

"Why can't girls just do what we tell you to?"

"Okay." She covers her eyes. Peeks. Then shuts 'em again.

"This one's for you." Up on my toes, I kiss her right cheek. "This is me apologizing for all the wrong I done you in middle school." I kiss her on the left cheek. Staring at her lips, moving in closer, I stop, and tell her how much I liked her back in middle school. That when I think about the right girl, sometimes I think about her. Maybe deep down inside Ashley knows it. Only, Maleeka can't hear what I'm saying, because it's me talking in my own head.

A girl's got the right to choose who she wants. To say no to whoever she wants to say no to. In her own way, Maleeka said no to me a long, long time ago. Ashley got her reasons for saying no too. I ain't wanna hear it, that's all. I got no choice now. Caleb either, when I think about it. His house is gone. So is his car, Maleeka too, probably. We both gotta learn to move on.

CHAPTER 87

IT'S DARK WHEN I hear Mom come into my room. It's late, like around the time the birds start with all that noise outside. She's sneaking in, tiptoeing. Trying not to wake me up. She would do that sometimes when I was in elementary school. Back then, I'd sit up, scared. "Mom, that you?" I always said.

This time I don't move or open my mouth. I know why she's here.

Mom couldn't be a spy. The hardwood floor is squeaking under her feet. She forgets where I leave my sneakers, and trips over 'em. Now she's talking to herself. "I tell him all the time . . . pick up after yourself. But does he?"

Even in the dark, she looks after me. I can see her bend down and walk my sneakers across the room. They get put where they should have been the first time, in my closet on the top shelf.

Mom comes and sits on the edge of my bed. I keep my eyes closed, stay stiff as a pencil, trying to fake sleep. She don't lay her hand on mine the way she did when I was little. And she doesn't pray out loud, the way I thought she might. Mom prays under her breath. I can't hear a word, just low whispers.

Is she asking God to look out for me? Thanking Him for

bringing me home like she do sometimes? Asking Him to find who done this to us?

"Amen," I hear her say after she's finished. On her way out, she stops by the door. "It's gonna happen fast . . . graduation . . . college. A wife, children. I ain't ready, God. Help me get ready. He'll be a man overnight."

I wanna get up and kiss her. Tell her I'm already a man. But she wouldn't understand.

CHAPTER 88

I'M GLAD SCHOOL hasn't started yet. I couldn't show up looking like this, people would run away from me. Standing in the living room mirror, I pull back my top lip, stare at my missing tooth. I won't be trying to talk to girls for a while.

I ignore the house phone when it rings. It's usually for Mom. But when it starts over for the third time in a row, I finally answer. "What you want, Caleb?"

He found his car, he says, sounding nervous. "If we hurry, we can go get it—now."

"We? You lucky I picked up the phone."

"My mother keeps asking me about it. I need it to take my father to the hospital. I told her your dad is putting new tires on it."

"Why you bring my dad into it?"

He doesn't have time to argue, he says. Am I coming or not? Caleb wants to know. I hang up on him. He calls right back, talking fast. When he brings up my father and says he might get him to help out, I get even madder. "He's done enough for you."

That shuts Caleb up. But neither one of us gets off the phone. He's breathing hard, mad I guess. I'm thinking about what my father said. You can't let somebody, not even a friend, get away with disrespecting you. So, I tell Caleb I'll meet him. But I'm not trying to find his car. I'm gonna finish what he started, even if I lose. Which I won't because he got lucky the last time.

CHAPTER 89

CALEB AND ME both get to Thirty-Seventh Street about the same time. Soon as I'm close enough, I do what I came to do—knock him down with one punch. Standing with my foot over his face, I tell him, "We're even now." Inside I just wanna stomp him to the ground. Smash his face in. But I ain't that kind of boy.

The hedges let us know we're getting close to the house where Caleb's car is. We don't have those around our way. Not many trees either. People in this neighborhood got 'em all, thick tall hedges, dark green, sharp as knives. Big houses and garages. But none of that keeps us from seeing Caleb's ride.

It's parked on the street in front of a house with yellow shutters and a navy-blue door. Somebody washed it. Waxed it. Detailed the rims.

We're in the street, by the car, when that blue door opens. A man with no hair, long legs, and a gray beard walks over to us like he's got combat boots on instead of flip-flops. "Y'all want something?"

Caleb explains in a real polite voice that the car belongs to him. He pulls papers out his wallet. Tries to make his fingers stop shaking. "I, I . . . have insurance coverage . . . my, my owner's registration . . . with me. See?"

The man is polite too. Says he bought the car two days ago. He has papers to prove it, he tells us. Not that he shows 'em. But if we want the car, he'll sell it to us for five thousand dollars, he says.

It's not worth that. Plus, he didn't pay that price either. He says so when Caleb asks. "You want it back? That's what it'll cost." A man's got a right to make a profit, he tells us.

This dude's like Dad, he lifts weights. He used to be a prison guard and thinks we ought to go home and forget about things. I almost ask if he knows my father. If he does, he might give Caleb his car back—no questions asked. Only, I can't do that. My father don't respect me, I see that now. He thinks I'm a goof-up, a kid, a weak little nerd with nothing going on. If me and Caleb gonna do this, it's got to be without his help.

"Let's leave, Caleb."

He's afraid, you can tell. But he don't move. Doesn't look up or shut up either. "It's my car and I want it."

Without saying nothing, the man goes back onto his property into the house. Caleb follows him, walks up to the door, knocks six times—hard. Then goes over to the window, staring in. That's when I run up to him.

The door opens. "Take your friend home," the man says. "I will only say it once."

When we get to Fifth and Caribe Lane, normally I would go my way and Caleb goes his way. Today, I say what I been thinking since we left that man. "How come boys like us don't ever win? The good ones, I mean. We're supposed to win some-time, ain't we?"

CHAPTER 90

SOON AS I got home, I knew we done the wrong thing leaving there empty-handed. Word gets around about something like that and you can't live it down. Might as well be in the ground, buried. Feels like I am sometimes anyhow. So, I call Caleb. "We going back. We have to."

I stay up all night thinking about Caleb and his dad and about what my father told me too. I can't always lose. What kind of girl wants a boy like that? I told Caleb what my father had said. We can't always be losers, punks, cowards. I added those last words 'cause all night long they kept jumping in my head like fleas on a dog, making it hard for me to sleep.

Ashley's mother wouldn't like what we're gonna do. Mom either. But a girl needs somebody to take up for her when the time comes. A boy who won't leave her if something bad happens. One who would take a arrow for her. I'm that dude, I wanna be anyhow.

The next Sunday, before Mom wakes up, I shower and put on boots and old clothes. I don't want my good stuff ruined. Stopping at the hallway mirror, I punch my chest and talk to myself. "Dad's gonna finally have a good story to tell about me for once."

CHAPTER 91

CALEB AIN'T AS brave as he was last week when we first came. Turning around, he says we should leave. Go back home. Forget about it. I'm beside him, looking back over my shoulder at that man's house. "It's not like your car is going anywhere, right? It don't look like he even moved it. Not once. Who buys a car, gets it detailed, and lets it sit day and night?"

We go around the corner. Sit on the first steps we get to. Sweat and think. Stink and sit quiet for a long time. I don't ask what he wanna do 'cause I ain't sure what I wanna do now. Leaving is on my mind though. Finally, Caleb brings up Maleeka. Did I see the second edition of her newspaper? he asks, pulling it out his pocket. It's folded small as a phone. "She wrote about us."

There's a column where girls send in questions they want answered. It's called Dear Maleeka. They ask her about dating, makeup, hair, bullying.

One section of the paper is about news from our neighborhood. *Good News*, she calls it. You got a birthday, anniversary, wedding, you get a shout-out in her paper. Miss Jeanie's daughter's picture is here with her new husband and baby.

On the other side, there's an obituary section. A ad from Dad. That ain't no surprise. A section called *Boys You Should*

Know. Now, that's a surprise. Especially when I see a picture of me by the bookmobile handing out books. How she get that? I almost ask. Maleeka mentions my grades, Mom's job, Dad about to win something from the Chamber, the good work me and the truck do, where people can send money or donate more books.

She talks about Caleb's father, how Caleb takes such good care of him, all the hours he puts in, colleges that are already writing Caleb about enrolling in their schools, his lawn-care business—why the world needs more boys like him and me.

"You think you and Maleeka will ever get back to—"

He shakes his head no. "I called her . . . this morning." Caleb wants her back, I can tell. But Maleeka says with all that's going on in her house and his, they should just be friends for now.

I think about Ashley. I like her. But she ain't ready for a boy like me, I see that now. I changed over the summer, Caleb too. Ashley's still the same, no different than she was in book club. I want a girl like Char or Maleeka. They make me laugh. They make me think. They don't let me get away with nothing, either. We changing all the time. Ashley's trying. But she ain't there yet. I want a girl who is.

CHAPTER 92

WE WALK ONTO his property, pass a black truck, stopping at Caleb's car. It's parked in front of his garage. Guess he moved it to keep it away from us. Two big, bright lights come on.

Caleb came with a extra key from home. But he's so nervous, he drops it. Picks it up and drops it again. I got it in my hand now. "Move." My fingers shake worse than his, but I get his car door open. For a minute, I think about Ashley. What if me and Caleb really are those boys her mother warned her about?

The alarm goes off in the car beside Caleb's. Windows go up across the street. The man who bought the car comes out the house, reaching into his pocket.

Backing up, Caleb hits the trash can and takes down a bike. On the street, he almost hits a cat, then goes through a stop sign doing sixty. I keep looking back.

"Nobody's coming," I say after a while. "They're not following us." I make myself breathe regular. Notice I got no seat belt on but don't do anything about it. When Caleb finally slows down, I close my eyes and laugh. Him too. "Nobody will believe we did this, nobody," I say.

He puts on his turn signal. "I don't believe it."

"Feels good, don't it?"

He nods, but not right away. "It's not . . . stealing."

"No, it's not. This car is yours. You have the papers."

"Yeah." He slaps the outside of the door with his hand, then drives with no hands. "Nobody is taking anything from me ever again."

I stand up. "Yeah. And don't be coming for us unless you want some of this!" I punch the air. Slap the windshield.

"Alright, John-John."

When I sit down, I put my feet out the window. That's when I remember my stuff. "Pull over."

"Why?"

"So I can check. They stole from me too, you know."

It's still here. My equipment. But the money and the phones are gone. Now Caleb's driving like we're on our way to a funeral.

CHAPTER 93

A TRUCK IS following us. It's that man, we know it. He got the high beams on. Beeps the horn like we're stupid enough to stop.

Caleb's foot pushes the pedal till it's flat. Till we going past park cars that look like they moving along with us.

That truck is fast. It's keeping up, almost catches up a bunch of times. But Caleb's car can do one-forty, only he's been afraid to test it out. He was doing ninety last time I looked.

I check my seat belt. Remember what Caleb said a little while ago about not telling his parents if something bad happened to him. But I got to make it home tonight. And all the nights for the rest of my life. My mother would never forgive herself if I didn't.

"Caleb, slow down!"

He got the car at a hundred now, driving straight up the highway with no turns. I pat his arm. Point to a exit sign saying two miles to Miller Park. He puts on his blinker, like that'll matter. Crosses four lanes quick as I can cross my fingers. Taps the brakes. Slows down, still takes the curves faster than he should.

That truck don't give up.

Caleb goes through another light. Two miles feels like one block, he's so quick. Finally, he turns into the park. The lights go off at ten p.m. to keep people out. So it's like we're drowning in the river with black everywhere. He slows down. Turns on his high beams. I blink. See shadows of trees big as houses. Tall as city hall. Roads that start but seem like they don't end 'cause it's so dark here. Caleb slows down some more, even when I say he shouldn't.

"I can't see."

He's doing twenty-five now.

"He's catching up."

His tire hits something, rocking the car like we're on a roller coaster. I open my case, load up. Next thing we know, we're caught. My hands so nervous I can't draw my bow. The truck stops, the window comes down. It's not that man who sticks his head out the window. It's T-One giving us the finger. "I told my brother it was y'all." Laughing, he calls us nerds. Says he wanted to see us wet our pants.

I did, a little.

CHAPTER 94

I DON'T MENTION my heart beating so hard I thought I'd drop dead on the spot. I'm quiet, like him, in the park, shooting in the dark, using his car for light. It don't last long. He's tired. Not me. I could stay up all night, I tell Caleb. On our way home, he takes the long way. Every once in a while, we laugh at what just happened.

"It feels good, don't it?" I say.

Caleb says he didn't know he had it in him to take curves at seventy miles an hour or stand up for himself. I ask if he's still mad at his father. Yes comes out of his mouth quick as spit. He's gonna talk to him though, he says. And let him know how he feels.

At my house, I get out the car feeling like a hero, different, brand-new. Not tired at all, I go up the alley, through the gate into our yard, wondering when they'll fix the light on our block. Soon as I get the key in the lock I take it out. Once I get in the house, Mom will wake up mad and put me on punishment. Might as well have my fun now.

I unzip my case. Load. Aim. Shoot toward the sky. Repeat. Freeze when I hear feet coming up the alley. I think about Mom and her group. What they been saying about parties, people we don't know in the alley. It gets quiet for a minute.

Then I hear feet again and think about that man who bought Caleb's car. What if he followed us anyhow? Saw me come back here?

I ain't scared this time, just ready. When I hear the latch opens, I shoot.

He hollers. "JJ!"

"Dad!"

CHAPTER 95

"YOU HAPPY NOW?" Mom's been walking back and forth since she got here. "You bought that thing for him—"

"Mom—"

". . . how come I'm just finding out that you the one responsible for him getting it in the first place?" I can hear the tears in her throat. "What . . . if . . . he killed you? Then I woulda lost him and . . ." For the first time since he left, she hugs him. Leans down and hugs him easy like, careful not to touch the bandages wrapped around his neck, the tubes in his arm.

He pats her back and whispers so it's hard to hear him now. But I hear him. "Sorry . . . It was stupid . . . what I did. Don't blame John."

Quick as she bent down, she's up, brushing her top and pants. Mom just needs to do something with her hands, I think. She steps around me and starts pacing again. I'm in the middle of the room, not sure what to do with myself since I walked in. It's this way every day. I come with Mom. Stand and stare awhile. Sit beside him until his wife comes. Then I start to leave. "Stay." Sheila says it every time. "I could use the company." I do. I feel guilty though. I shot my father. Who does that?

It wasn't the arrow that hurt him the worst. It was the fall. He hit his head, cracked his skull on the ground. He ended up with a concussion. My arrow hit him in the neck, near a artery. He tripped over his feet. Hit the ground so hard we heard it shake.

"Leave the boy alone," he tells Mom.

"How could you ever think it was a good idea?" Mom says.

His wife said the same thing yesterday. "We almost lost you, Big John. And for what?" She did that rubbing thing. "So you could make a man out of him? Don't you ever do try that with my son."

Mom shakes her head. "Now John is in the newspaper for something silly."

At least I won't have a record. Dad said to tell the police I didn't know who was in the alley. That part was true anyhow. That I tripped on my way out the gate and the arrow shot off by itself. That part wasn't. I walk over to my father and sit beside him. Before she leaves, Mom tells me to be home by seven.

"You need your pillow raised?" I stand up. "Ice in your water?" I get the little plastic pitcher off the table and open the lid. "Oh. No, you got plenty." I'm sitting back down when I go through channels on TV. His eyes open, close, open close. In between, he smiles at me. When he wiggles his fingers, I know what that means. Reaching over, I hold his hand. Squeeze it, just not too hard. "You can go to sleep. I ain't going nowhere."

It's six when he finally wakes up this time. "JJ?"

"I'm here."

"Can I get some water?" He licks his dry lips.

"Sure." I find a straw in a drawer. I lower the rail and crank the head of the bed up higher. After that, I hold the cup while he drinks.

"Tastes good. Thanks."

We're quiet for a while. Then he starts explaining. He knows everybody in this neighborhood, he says. "Nothing don't happen unless I know." But this time, he didn't until Mom called him, saying it was almost two and she was worried about where I was.

Mom and him called around, starting with kids I went to school with, he says. "We couldn't find out anything." Finally, he told her to go to sleep. After he didn't have any luck finding me, he came back to our house. "I always liked to sit on the back porch, remember?"

"Yeah."

"That's what I was gonna do. Sit and wait for you to come home." He squeezes my hand. "Your momma can't sleep if she don't know where you're at." He whispers. "Me either."

Mom's been asking where I was and what I was doing that night I shot my father. I told her me and Caleb were in the park practicing. That was some of the truth. Dad knew it wasn't the whole truth. He asks again for like the tenth time since he got admitted, for me to tell him what we were up to. "I'll find out anyhow."

I tell him everything, including how good it felt shooting arrows in the dark, shutting my eyes.

"You know that's a bad idea, right?"

"Now I do."

I talk about wanting my curfew changed. Walking back and

forth, I mention how different I feel now. Stronger. Taller. "Maybe I should take boxing classes." I throw hands. Duck, throw again, jab. I don't notice how he's looking at me till I sit down to catch my breath. "What?" I hold up my fists. "I do it wrong? The uppercut or the lower cut?"

"I'm too old for this." He laughs, but it's a sad one, tired too. I shoulda came to him, he says, about the car, about everything.

I remind Dad what he said about winning. I tell him he was right, it feels good not to lose all the time. I wanna get a whole lot more used to not losing too, I say. "That's why I wanna take boxing lessons. You know Mom took my equipment and threw it into the river? If you get me another set, I won't tell."

He's staring at me like he don't know who I am.

"You hear me, Dad?"

His eyes water. He rubs the spot on his neck where he got hit. "I thought you meant it for me. That you wanted me gone . . . and did it on purpose."

"I wouldn't do that."

He holds on to my hand. "I know." He quits talking to wipe his face. "I feel like the worst father on earth."

"But you're not . . . and I never said you were."

"I talk about being old. But on that ground, blood everywhere, I thought about you, your brother and sister with no father, and I was praying, boy. I was praying not to die."

I bend over and hug him, careful not to hurt him.

"Love you, boy. You my son. Don't you ever forget that."

"I won't."

Dad don't talk about his own father much. Lying here, he

tells me how his dad always compared him to other boys. "I always hated it. Said I'd never do it to my son. Then I did."

He asks if I can help him take a walk up the hall. Pushing his IV pole while he walks, my father tells me that I've always been a good boy. Never any trouble. Never broke the law, not even my curfew. "That's the son I want."

"But you always said—"

"You ain't me. And I ain't you. Took an arrow in the neck to see that."

In the ambulance, he says, all he could think of was that I was going to jail, getting locked up, and it would have been all his fault.

"You didn't tell me to shoot it, Dad."

"I gave it to you."

"I wanted it."

"I told you to lie about it to your mother."

"It wasn't the first time I lied to her."

It wasn't just the lie, it was everything, he says, like me sneaking off to get the car, fighting Caleb all summer, breaking curfew, changing.

"I thought you wanted me to change."

He stops at the window at the end of the hall and sits in a chair. "I never said that."

"It's what you meant." I lean against the wall, listening to him breathe.

"Am I a bad father?"

"No. I'm growing up."

He looks at me, examining my face. "You checking for bumps?" I ask.

"No, I'm checking for you." He keeps looking. I don't turn away. "Yeah, you changed alright," Dad says.

But that don't mean I don't need him, I say. "And that you can't talk to me."

"Talk to you? So you real grown now, huh?"

"Dad, you know what I mean."

"Nobody wants to hear what I have to say."

"Maybe if you say it the right way, they just might. Anyhow, I want to know about your knee."

"Know what?"

"You scared to get it operated on, huh?"

He don't answer. I tell him I was scared of girls, and now I ain't. At least that's something Ashley did for me.

He's rubbing his knee. "It's a long surgery, anesthesia and everything. I make the money in the house. If it goes wrong . . ." He rubs it again. "People get blood clots, doctors make mistakes . . . I got a baby coming, you know."

I listen and listen, surprised how long he talks.

CHAPTER 96

DRESSED IN A suit, I walk in Caleb's house. My father forgot something and he needs it for the speech he's giving at the Chamber in two hours. "I'll be a while," he tells me. "Want me to drop you off at home?"

Take me to Caleb's, I say. Mr. P. just got out of the hospital. Two weeks after school started, they took him there in an ambulance. He had a stroke, a little one. Been in the hospital for a month now. The move was pushed back for a couple of weeks.

"You look good, Mr. P.," I say, walking into his bedroom. "Not as good as me though in this suit." I turn around, spinning on my heels.

He's on the other side of the room, in the new leather recliner his brothers pitched in to get, he tells me. "Nice, huh, John?"

"Sure is."

He gained some weight, I can tell. Worked on the way he speaks so he don't sound like a robot as much.

"The hospital was like a, a, vacation . . . for my body and my brain," he says.

"Maybe I should go there," I say.

I could use some work on my brain, Caleb tells me. Then

he asks his dad if it's too cold with the air conditioner on. "If it is, I can get you a—"

"I'll, I'll get it." Mr. P. uses a cane now. But he's walking a lot better, that's good. He says he'll be running a marathon soon. But he's out of breath once he gets to the closet. Caleb asks if he needs help and gets turned down. "They. Want. Me. To try harder."

Opening the closet door, he picks out a gray sweater and puts it on, all by himself. Yeah, it takes him a minute. But he does it. "I was giving up."

We knew, but we didn't say we knew.

"Selling the house. Made me feel. Like. I. Was. Contributing. Keeping. My family safe." But it wasn't right not to consider their feelings, he says.

I asked Caleb if he still was mad at his dad. Not as much as he was when their house first got sold, he told me last week. "But sometimes when I really, really think about it, I get mad all over again. Furious." He sees a counselor at school once a week now. He works for Dad on Saturdays, organizing all that junk in his garage. I see him and Maleeka together at school, even though they say they're not together.

Mr. P. is in his seat when he asks Caleb to hand him the green folder in his suitcase downstairs. Caleb's gone and back in no time. His dad pulls out a page full of exercises, a list of medicines and schedules for the physical therapist, the real nurse, and his visits with the psychologist. They found a program to cover a lot of the costs, his mother said.

I sit up. "What they trying to say about you, Mr. P.?"

"That I suffer from . . . depression." He holds up a bottle

of pills. Picks up another sheet of paper. It's another schedule. One he came up with hisself. Every day for two hours he'll be in his office working, he tells us.

But you ain't got no job, I wanna say.

He'll have one someday, he says, like he can read my mind. In the meantime, he's gonna work on his resume, reach out to friends, and learn to be patient. "I'm not . . . done living yet."

"Now don't rush it." Caleb's mom walks in carrying a tray full of food. "They said for you to pace yourself. You're still healing, you know."

Mr. P. says, "Our whole family is."

When it's time for me to go, Caleb walks me to the door. "I saw Ashley." He sits on the rocker. "You still like her?"

"A little."

But I got other things to do now. I'm starting a after-school book club with my old elementary school. And I'm talking to this girl. I like her a lot. Not saying who she is. But Maleeka and Caleb know her. With my big mouth, I might ruin it. So I'm not saying nothing.

"You good?" I say, right when my father shows up beeping his horn.

"Yeah. We're moving soon. I'm applying to business schools for next year, so I won't live there long." He wants to start a business while he's in college, he says. "I still want to be rich."

"Who don't?" I say.

CHAPTER 97

WALKING UP THE steps to the Chamber of Commerce, I start to sweat. Dad stops me. "Let me take a look at you." He straightens my tie. Lifts my jacket sleeves one at a time, checking my cuffs. "Your turn is coming, son. Watch and see."

I was going to invite Caleb to come. But Dad said he wanted it to be me and him, if I didn't mind. He's been trying to spend more time with me doing things I want to do. Which means Home Depot is out, gone, finally. Not that I get to do archery. But we've been to a few baseball games, two museums, and we eat at places I want to eat at now. "I got to work up to gladiators," my father told me.

In the lobby, a guard signs us in. Then he walks us over to elevators that look like they're made out of gold. There's eight in all, four on each side. Some go to the thirtieth floor, the penthouse, he says. You don't have to push your own buttons once you get on, because somebody does it for you. "I could get used to this," I say.

A girl in the elevator reminds me of Ashley. Since I'm not in book club, I don't see her much. But she heard about me and Caleb, she said, the second day of school. It's not like I'm over her. But I'm over her, know what I mean? Char helped. I liked Ashley more than she liked me. And I liked her mostly because

I've been wanting somebody to like me and be my girlfriend for a long time. I don't wanna be that boy anymore. I'm *not* that boy anymore.

I open the door for my father. He steps aside and lets me go in first.

ACKNOWLEDGMENTS

I want to thank readers around the globe who have walked this journey with me for twenty-five-plus years. I'd also like to welcome new readers and fans into a world like no other, where my much-beloved characters—John-John, Caleb, Maleeka, and Char—manage to hold on to the hearts, imaginations, curiosity, and trust of readers from the first page of the book to the last.

I could not have done this work without Scholastic, who, along with my editor, Andrea Davis Pinkney, give me the support and creative freedom I need to tell authentic stories about Black youth—stories that stay in the hearts and minds of readers long after they have their own children, or become educators and other specialists, working tirelessly to impact the lives of children everywhere.

Lastly, thanks to my agent, Jennifer Lyons of the Jennifer Lyons Agency. Authors need agents who believe in them and their work, and who can put their books in the right hands. I am glad to also have you walk this journey beside me.

ABOUT THE AUTHOR

As the prolific author of numerous books, SHARON G. FLAKE's novels have brought a bold dimension to literature for young people, selling more than a million copies world-wide, and reaching readers across the globe through numerous translations and theatrical productions. Ms. Flake's impressive body of work includes dozens of novels, chapter books, and illustrated works. She is the recipient of multiple Coretta Scott King Author Honor Awards and is a Kirkus Award nominee. Ms. Flake has received numerous NAACP Image Award nominations, among other citations, and has been praised as one of the single most influential authors of teen works whose novels have inspired a pantheon of writers. To learn more, please visit sharongflake.com.